A Song for Silas

LORI WICK

HARVEST HOUSE PUBLISHERS
Eugene, Oregon 97402

A SONG FOR SILAS

Copyright © 1990 by Harvest House Publishers
Eugene, Oregon 97402

Library of Congress Cataloging-in-Publication Data

Wick, Lori.
    A song for Silas / Lori Wick.
    Sequel to: A place called home.
    ISBN 1-56507-589-7
    I. Title.
PS3573.I237H6   1990
813'.54—dc20

90-33476
CIP

98 99 00 01 02 / BC / 14 13 12 11 10 9

To Mary Vesperman,
secretary and dear friend.
I couldn't have done it
without you.

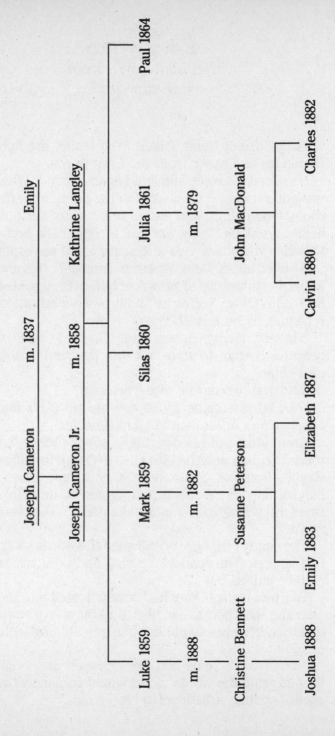

CAMERON FAMILY TREE
1889

FOREWORD
Neillsville, Wisconsin
February 1889

"Amy!" Grant Nolan called from inside the house and waited for an answer from the front porch.

He raised his voice and tried again. "*Amy!*" When there was still no answer, he walked to the porch from the living room. Grant stood and stared at his daughter a moment before speaking. "Amy, are you alright?" His brows drew together in a sharp V as she again failed to respond.

He tried again. "Amy, where is Thomas?" Grant watched as his daughter turned to look at him as though seeing him for the first time. Seeing he finally had her attention, Grant repeated, "Where is Thomas?"

"He left." Her voice was oddly flat and she turned her head once again to stare out into the yard at nothing in particular.

"Did you two have a disagreement?"

"No, he just came by to tell me he can't marry me because he's in love with Debra Wheeler."

Grant stared at his daughter's sober profile. The wind tossed her hair and she lifted her left hand to remove a few strands from her cheek. Grant's eyes were drawn to that hand. Empty. He felt his throat tighten at Amy's loss of the small ruby ring which had belonged to Thomas Blane's mother.

The empty ring finger confirmed the words his daughter had spoken. The sparkle the ring had brought was completely snuffed out.

Two months ago Amy had nearly floated into the house after she and Thomas had been on a Sunday afternoon ride together, her eyes sparkling, her face shining with happiness.

"Dad." Amy's voice had been hushed as though afraid that uttering the words aloud would somehow break the spell. "Thomas asked me to marry him."

She then had held out her left hand to show the lovely ruby set in a thin gold band. "It was his mother's, and he wants me to wear it so the world will know I am his."

Staring at his daughter with a mixture of emotions, Grant had risen to take her in his arms. Pain had mingled with overwhelming joy as he realized that his daughter had grown up and found a Christian man to spend her life with—his sorrow was over the fact that her mother wasn't there to see and share this special moment.

As though able to read her father's thoughts, Amy had raised her eyes to meet the loving ones above her. "I feel like Mother can see us and we have her blessing." Grant could only nod, his heart overflowing with joy for his daughter.

But now that peace had been shattered in a moment's time. Grant struggled to control his feelings of anger at the thought that anyone would reject his daughter. She had suffered more than enough pain and loss in her young life.

He knew some adults who would not have stood as strong as she had. But Amy was special, gifted and loving, taking each blow in stride, as she placed her small hand in the all-encompassing grasp of Jesus Christ as He had led the way through the dark tunnels of pain. Emerging from each trial more refined, Amy grew stronger and lovelier with every passing year.

Realizing he was still just standing and staring at Amy, Grant noticed absently the way the sun turned her golden hair to a fiery glow. As he walked to join his daughter on the porch swing, he prayed, wanting to comfort but not to intrude. He asked God to help Amy turn to her Lord for comfort as she had always done in the past.

As Grant shifted and settled his weight on the swing, Amy reached for his hand. Father and daughter sat side by side and were comforted with one another's presence.

Grant Nolan knew without a trace of prejudice that his daughter was the most wonderful one in the world. "Please God," he prayed silently, "please let Your will for Amy be as special as she is."

1

Baxter, Wisconsin
April 1889

Luke Cameron rolled onto his side to better see the little person in bed with him: his son ... six months old ... Joshua Luke Cameron. Luke's eyes moved over the cap of dark curls and down to the fan of equally dark lashes that lay still in sleep.

Joshua slept with his chest against the mattress and his little round bottom in the air, one tiny fist pushed into his flushed cheek.

It had been last year, Luke reflected, when Christine was still pregnant, that he and Mac had been talking on Grandma Em's front porch. Mac's words came back to him as he looked at the miracle of his son. "God is still faithful even amid our foolishness."

September 1888

John MacDonald stretched and flexed his massive back and shoulders, causing the chair on Grandma Em's porch to creak in protest. Luke Cameron was settled on the porch railing, letting the afternoon sun warm his back. It was warm for September—Indian summer—but no one was complaining. The snow would be upon them soon enough.

Mac, short for MacDonald, watched as his two sons, Calvin and Charles, charged out of the house. He followed their progress as they raced down the front porch steps and off to the willow tree to swing on some of the bare switches. His face reflected the pride he felt.

"It's hard to believe Cal is nine years old." Luke nodded as he also followed the progress of the boys—his nephews— as they raced around in the autumn sun.

"What's even more amazing," Mac replied, "is all your sister went through to get him here."

9

"I don't remember Julia having a hard time with labor and delivery," Luke answered, with a puzzled look on his face.

"She didn't have a hard time having Cal, just carrying him, and I'm afraid it was all my fault."

Luke stared at his brother-in-law, wondering what in the world he was talking about. Mac met Luke's stare and confessed, "I was scared to death for Julia to have Calvin."

Luke squirmed a bit at hearing these words. They so closely echoed his own thoughts now that Christine, his wife, was nearly seven months along with their first child.

Mac, seeming not to notice Luke's discomfort, went on. "Julia was over six months along before I realized she knew I was scared." Mac shook his head at the remembrance.

"Everything was fine with Julia and the baby and she knew it, but to give me peace of mind she worked twice as hard as she needed, carefully not showing me her exhaustion and never complaining about the way her body ached. But I didn't see any of it. The worst part was, I stopped touching her. I was afraid that if I even hugged her, I'd hurt the baby. Julia was over two-thirds of the way into her pregnancy, and I had never even felt the baby move. I can't believe how much I missed. She was working like a horse, and I was treating her as though she were made of glass. She told me later she had never been so hurt, thinking I was repulsed by her pregnant shape."

Mac again shook his head at his own stupidity. "Sometimes God allows us to go through some painful times. But we learned from it, and the rest of Julia's pregnancy was wonderful. God is still faithful even amid our foolishness."

Later that night, Luke knew he had to confront his wife. The lamp was blown out, and Luke lay in the darkness gathering courage to speak, knowing if he waited too long Christine would fall asleep. Wordlessly he moved and took her into his arms. Christine was so surprised by this action that for a few minutes she uttered not a sound, but lay in tense silence. When was the last time Luke had held her like this? How many times had she begged God, "Please, Lord, let Luke's affection for me return after the baby is born"?

But his touching her so suddenly like this was not a comfort. Her back began to ache with the tense way she held herself, waiting for whatever bad news he must have to tell her. When she could no longer stand it, she asked in a shaky voice, "Luke, is something wrong?"

Luke knew this was his chance. She was waiting and ready. All he had to do was explain to her about his fear and how much he loved and wanted to take care of her. But Luke decided foolishly not to burden her with all his fears. "No, Christine, everything is fine."

The next week was torture for both husband and wife. Luke, having decided to show Christine how he felt, only managed to confuse her by the change in his behavior. By Sunday of the next week, Christine's confusion had turned to anger and, after serving breakfast, she had quietly informed her husband she would not be going to church that day.

Christine was in the bedroom when she heard the horses move away pulling the wagon, so she was very surprised to hear someone walking down the hall.

Luke stopped just inside the doorway and found his wife in the rocker by the stove. Her eyes met his for just an instant before returning to the mending in her lap. "I thought you went to church with Si."

"You're angry." It was a statement and not a question.

"What makes you think that?" Christine asked as she viciously jabbed the needle into the shirt in her hands.

"Christine, we've got to talk."

Something in her husband's tone made Christine look up. Their eyes met and she knew he was as miserable as she. What followed were hours of soul-baring. Fear, pride, anger, hurt—they all were confessed to each other and then to God. The fear Luke had felt about losing Christine in childbirth, and the rejection Christine felt because of that fear, turned to love and new commitment.

Later, as Luke's hands lay on Christine's stomach feeling their child move within, Mac's words came back: "God is still faithful even amid our foolishness."

— ✣ —

The sound of booted feet coming down the hall brought Luke back to the present. He rolled to his back and watched his wife enter the room.

Christine Cameron, even in denim jeans and a man's shirt, was poised and lovely. Luke smiled at the sight of her.

She sat down on the edge of the bed and leaned to kiss her husband.

"Did I wake you?"

"No."

Husband and wife spoke in hushed tones even though they knew it was unnecessary. The high activity level of their son caused him to sleep deeply whenever he slowed down long enough to let slumber claim him. Saturday had developed into a routine of Luke and Josh taking a nap together giving Christine a bit of free time. Most days she went riding with Julia.

Christine reached across her husband to tenderly pat her son's bottom. She smiled as he moved and shoved his balled-up fist into his mouth.

"You weren't out for very long. Would you care to join us?"

Luke's inviting smile was tempting. The bed was plenty big enough to hold them but she felt dusty from her ride. Luke saw her hesitation and began to pull gently on her arm. Christine had just settled comfortably in Luke's embrace when they heard the front door open and close.

"Anybody home?"

Luke and Christine were out of bed in a flash upon hearing that deep voice from the living room. Silas was home.

2

Chicago, Illinois

Silas Cameron stared in stunned silence at the man across from him. The beautiful book-lined study with its elegant chairs and tables faded from view. He couldn't believe Frank Chambers had just asked him to come and work for him.

"I can see you're surprised, Silas, but I can assure you the offer is genuine." The older man's voice was slightly amused.

"Surprised is putting it mildly, Frank, and I'm very flattered but..."

"No, no, Silas. I don't want an answer right now," Frank cut him off. "You owe it to Luke as your partner, as well as your brother, to discuss it with him. I also realize the thought of leaving Baxter has probably never occurred to you, so I want you to give it some time. Think on it. I'll tell you exactly what I have in mind, and after you go home, I'll wait a few weeks to deliver your horses. I'll get your answer after I get to Baxter."

Frank then went on to explain the position in detail. Captivated, Silas listened closely.

"I delivered your horses last year because I liked Luke immediately upon meeting him, as well as all he had to say about his home. But, it is not normally my job. You can understand our operation here is too big for me to handle all the traveling."

"You deliver all the horses you sell?"

"Yes, we do. It has always been our policy. There have been a few times over the years when I have returned with the horses. No amount of money will make me leave my animals in a place where I feel they will be mistreated. I realize this is an unusual concept, but I've never been sorry and my reputation has been all the healthier for it." There was no boasting in his tone as he stated these facts, just a certainty he was doing the right thing. Considering the success of the Chambers' stables, Silas couldn't help but agree.

"What I have in mind for you is to deliver to our special customers. You have a calm way about you and can deliver our most valuable animals with the utmost care. Of this I'm sure. You would be traveling all over the United States and abroad probably at least once a year."

"Abroad? As in Europe?"

"Right! As I say, it's not very often, about once a year, but the job needs someone with your skill."

Frank talked on as Silas listened. He explained the other duties he had in mind and, when he named a salary, Silas had to work at keeping his mouth closed.

Silas went to bed with visions of travel and money floating through his head. He did not sleep well.

As Silas expected, Frank brought the matter up again on the way to the train station the following morning.

"There is one more thing I want you to understand, Silas. The salary I named is completely above and beyond any travel expenses you may have. We, of course, pay train fares for both you and the horses, and any time you must stay the night we'll cover that bill.

"Also, Silas, I am not insensitive to the close bond in your family. Anytime you are in the Baxter area with nothing urgent pressing here, you are more than welcome to stop and see them for a few days."

Silas was aware that Frank was talking as if he'd already accepted the job. It made him uncomfortable, and he was glad when the train station came into sight.

Frank's parting words as Silas stepped on the train were, "Think on it, Silas. I'll be up in a few weeks." Again, Silas had the impression Frank was already sure of the answer.

As the train moved along at a steady pace, the restless night began to catch up to Silas. He settled in and was nearly asleep when a child's crying woke him.

Across the aisle sat a woman with an infant and a toddler. The woman and the baby in her arms were fast asleep. The woman appeared to be literally limp with exhaustion. On the seat beside her was a little girl in a panic because she couldn't rouse her mother or fit into her already-full lap. Silas moved to the edge of his seat and held out his arms. There was a moment's hesitation, and then the little girl was in his arms.

With some coaxing, he discovered her name was Laura and that she was thirsty. When the tears were all dried and the thirst was quenched, Silas found her mother still sleeping, so he settled Laura in his lap.

Playing first with his tie and then his beard, Laura entertained him for the next hour, all the time talking to him in not-quite-recognizable English. When he asked her age, three little fingers went proudly into the air. Laura's head had just dropped onto Silas' chest when her mother awoke. Silas would have liked to prevent the frantic look he saw in her eyes before spotting her daughter, but he didn't want to move and wake Laura. He assured her in a quiet voice that Laura was fine where she was and, after giving Silas a grateful smile, the young mother settled back in her seat to feed the baby.

With all of the thoughts Frank Chambers had put into his head, Silas, strangely enough, found his thoughts turning to the child in his lap—not specifically Laura, but children in general. Silas had two nieces and three nephews whom he adored. But lately it was not enough. He had begun to ache for a home of his own, with a wife and children to fill his heart and life.

He even knew the exact place he would build his house. It was not far from Luke and Christine's, and the group of big oaks that stood on that spot would give a feeling of privacy to both homes. He and Luke had talked about it just last month. Luke had been all for it as long as Silas didn't feel as though he and Christine no longer wanted him with them. Silas had assured him this was not the case.

Now Silas' thoughts turned to Chicago and the job with Frank Chambers. It would save him the cost of building a home. Frank had a two-bedroom cottage not far from the main house and had said the rent would be a part of Silas' salary.

Silas shook his head as though trying to clear it, and Laura stirred. She sat up and spoke a few words to him before noticing her mother was awake. Silas' lap was deserted quickly and he once again settled in for a nap.

The remainder of the trip was uneventful, and Silas was relieved to step onto the platform at Baxter. Greetings from townsfolk enveloped him as he made his way to the livery. As planned, Luke had left a horse for him. Within a half hour of leaving the train station, Silas was headed to the ranch.

As he rode through the familiar surroundings, Silas couldn't help asking himself, "Could I actually leave all this?" Baxter was the only home Silas had ever known.

The ranch hadn't changed in two weeks, although Silas halfway expected it would because it seemed to him he'd been gone forever.

No one came out as he rode up, and it was so quiet he wondered if anyone was home. He wished for an instant that he'd stopped at Grandma Em's. Maybe everyone was there.

The smells were familiar as he stepped into the front room. He smiled. The aroma of whatever pie Christine had served for lunch still lingered in the air. Home. Silas couldn't believe it felt so good. As he quietly closed the door behind him, he called out, "Anybody home?"

3

Barely finishing a piece of pie and cup of coffee, Silas began answering questions. Luke and Christine wanted to know everything. Their first questions were about Paul, the youngest brother in the Cameron family, who was at seminary in Chicago.

Silas, understanding their concern for the brother they missed so much and saw so little of, started right in.

"Paul is great. He misses everyone but loves school. He fills a different pulpit in the area nearly every week. He also told me that as much as he loves his studies, there is no feeling in the world like that of preaching a sermon. I couldn't believe how excited he was."

"Do you think he'll take a church in the Chicago area when he graduates?" Christine wanted to know.

"Somehow I don't think he will. He's still too much in love with small-town life. But then again, he said this weekend that God has been teaching him a lot about surrendering his will to God's. His most fervent prayer is that he, Paul Cameron, will be God's man for the job."

"When does he think he'll be home again?" Luke couldn't keep the wistfulness out of his voice. It seemed like forever since he had sat down and talked with his youngest brother.

Silas looked apologetic as he answered. "I wouldn't watch for him until sometime this summer."

Further conversation was interrupted by a small cry from the direction of the bedroom. When Christine rose, Silas stopped her. "Sit down, Christine. I've been waiting patiently for that sound since I walked in the door. I need to see my little Josh." Silas threw a beaming smile at Luke and Christine before moving to get his nephew.

Joshua Cameron always had a smile for his Uncle Silas. Always, that is, except for today. Silas scooped him off his

17

parents' bed to hug and kiss him hello, but Joshua just stared at the bearded face above him. Silas was not too surprised when Joshua's little arms reached for Christine as soon as he saw her.

Completely unoffended, Silas headed for the piano. He played a few quick notes and then held his arms out to his nephew. Joshua's smile was his reward and soon both were seated in their usual positions on the piano bench.

Completely hemmed in, Joshua was snuggled onto the piano bench with Silas' stomach at his back, the keyboard at his front, and Silas' arms stretched out on either side to reach the keys.

Silas never played from sheet music while Joshua was in his lap. He watched the little hands pound the keys in front of him or reach to the hands so much bigger than his own as they moved over the keys. If Joshua was especially tired, he would simply lay back against Silas and listen. Not so today. Fully revived from his nap, Joshua was ready to go.

The remainder of the afternoon flew by as Silas settled back into his home. When Joshua had been put to bed, Silas brought up to Luke and Christine the offer from Frank Chambers. They were as stunned as he had been. Christine had to bite her tongue to keep from coming right out and telling Silas he simply couldn't go. They talked for some time and Silas told them honestly he wasn't sure what he was supposed to do.

Knowing it would be best to sleep on it and do some more thinking and praying, Silas retired early. As he lay waiting for sleep to come, he knew he wanted God's will. But if he were completely honest, he also knew he hated to leave home, even for a short time. Coming home just felt so right. He asked God before he slept, If submitting to His will meant changing homes, would it ever feel as right as this one did?

The next day was Sunday and Silas awoke looking forward to church and then lunch with the family. He wanted very much to share the news of the job offer with the rest of the family and to ask for their advice and prayers. But as it was, the subject never came up.

Pastor Nolan had finished the closing prayer, but before dismissing the congregation, he spoke again. "Before I dismiss you this morning I would ask a few minutes of your time. Our niece Amy has written us to say that my brother has broken his leg." He paused as a ripple of murmurs moved across the room. "As most of you know, my brother has a farm in Neillsville where I grew up. I would ask for your prayers for Grant and Amy. A farmer's schedule does not allow for being laid up like this. I'm writing them tomorrow, and I'd like to tell them you are praying."

When the service was dismissed, Silas had to wait his turn to talk with the pastor. The men shook hands for a long moment before speaking, giving Silas time to see the lines of strain around the older man's eyes and mouth.

"I'm sure you know why I stayed to talk with you. Would I be out of line to ask if you can share more with me than you did from the pulpit?"

"It would be a relief to talk with you, Silas. Just let me see the rest of these folks out and I'll be right with you."

Silas was seated back in a pew but a few minutes when Mrs. Nolan joined him. "Thank you for staying, Silas."

"You know I'll do all I can." She met his assurance with a nod and they waited for the pastor in silence. When Pastor Nolan was finally seated, a conversation seasoned with the warmth of time began.

"The letter from Amy came yesterday. She wrote that Grant fell from a ladder and broke his leg. She also writes that the doctor has given him medicine for the pain and that he is completely bedridden. They haven't even started the planting. The letter went on to say that Amy is doing all the milking and she will be pulling money from their savings to pay for some help with the fields." Silas could hear the worry in Pastor Nolan's voice.

"Where is Evan?" Silas' voice was a bit angered.

"Nothing has changed with Evan. He never goes to the farm or anywhere near Grant. It's been four years. I have my doubts as to whether he'll ever get over Maureen's death. He's never said, but it's obvious he blames my brother for his sister's death."

They sat in silence for some minutes before Silas spoke. "When you write, tell them I'm coming."

"Are you sure, Silas? You've only just returned." The pastor's voice held genuine concern, but his eyes were hopeful.

"I'm sure." Silas spoke in a firm voice and in short order explained his plans and was on his way to see his family for the first time in two weeks, his heart a bit heavy at having to tell them he was leaving again.

4

Walking to Grandma Em's house from the church stirred up a bittersweet feeling in Silas. He knew that before the next Sunday dawned in Baxter, he would be on a small farm in Neillsville, Wisconsin, some 85 miles from his home.

As Silas walked up Grandma Em's street, he savored the approaching spring. It was his favorite time of year. He liked to pray for new growth in his own life as he watched the flowers come alive and the trees sprout new leaves. The weather was a bit chilly and the new growth really hadn't started yet, but there was a feeling of anticipation in the air, as though the plants and trees themselves knew something was about to happen.

Silas reflected a bit on the family with whom he was going to stay. Grant and Amy Nolan. Four years ago, upon the request of Pastor Nolan, Silas had gone to help Grant with his fall harvesting. Grant's wife, Maureen, had died suddenly and both Grant and his 14-year-old daughter, Amy, were in shock.

Amy. Silas smiled. The sweetest little girl Silas had ever met. Not demonstrative and very quiet, she had grieved silently, keeping to herself in a way that was heartbreaking. She had not spoken over five words to Silas the first week he was there. But in time the ice had melted and they became close, despite the 10 years difference in their ages.

They had not corresponded through the years, but Silas had kept abreast of the family through Mrs. Nolan. Grant had not remarried and Amy had been engaged but that was off now. She would be 18 now—a grown woman. Silas found himself hoping, as he climbed the steps to Grandma Em's front porch, that Amy would be as sweet as he remembered.

Sunday dinner was on the table and Mac had just prayed when Silas opened the front door. There was a round of hugs and kisses before everyone settled back down to the meal.

Silas had been all set to tell his family about his plans, but he was sitting next to his niece Emily, and she didn't let him get in a syllable. She questioned him thoroughly about Paul and then moved on to the horses.

"Did you get horses?"

"I sure did."

"What color are they? Can I ride one?"

Silas wasn't going to touch that one. He shot a look to Emily's mother, Susanne, but all she did was smile at him. No help there. A glance back at Emily told him she was awaiting his answer. Her eyes turned to him with hopeful anticipation. He knew he had to tell her the truth.

"I can't promise you a ride right now, sweetheart, because I have to go away again." As Silas expected, this statement captured everyone's attention. He might have been surprised to find out they had suspected this when, after church, he'd told Luke to take the buggy and that he'd walk to Grandma Em's.

"When do you leave?" The question was directed to him by his grandmother. He met her understanding eyes before looking at Luke to answer. "I was hoping Friday, but Luke and I have yet to talk."

Luke nodded and the meal progressed. The subject of Silas' departure was dropped, everyone realizing that Silas and Luke would have to talk this out on their own.

The front porch ended up hosting the conversation between the brothers. Luke's twin brother, Mark, and Mac were also present. Silas told them the added information Pastor Nolan had relayed, and concern was evident on every man's face for the trials of this family.

"How long do you expect to be gone?" Luke's question was matter-of-fact, knowing Silas' decision to go was already firmly planted in his mind.

"I could tell you a couple of weeks, but that's what I said last time and was gone for six." Silas was on the verge of saying more, but Luke cut in. "Actually, Si, I don't know why I ask you. I think your decision to go is just exactly that—your decision. I also know you have not made this decision lightly. I know we'll miss you, but we'll manage."

"I was thinking the same thing," Mark spoke now. "Why wait until Friday? The Nolans need you right now and we can help at the ranch whenever Luke gets into a bind, unlikely as that is."

Silas felt great relief at how supportive his family had been, until his sister-in-law Christine appeared. One look at the men on the porch told Christine the matter was all settled.

"Just like that. It's all settled isn't it?" No one said a word. "You've only just returned and you're leaving again." Her voice was not angry—resigned and sad, but not angry. "Well," Christine's voice had changed to determination just that fast, "if you don't write to us at least once a week, don't bother to come home."

The tension was broken at this and Silas moved to give Christine a hug, thinking as he did, what a relief it was to be leaving with his family's blessing.

5

"Did you write to Frank?" The question came from Luke as he and Silas headed toward the train station.

"Yes, I wrote. But if I know Frank, he'll not accept my answer."

Luke asked no more, fairly certain what Silas' answer had been. The train was a bit late, giving the men some time to talk. Silas seemed a bit edgy, and Luke couldn't keep from commenting on it. "Is anything bothering you, Si?"

Silas' answer did not come immediately. He was feeling very unsure of what he would find once he got to Neillsville, and he didn't want to burden Luke. In an instant he decided against it. "I'm just thinking ahead about my trip to the farm. I've got a long day ahead of me." All of which was true.

Luke noticed the evasive answer but only said, "I hear the train. Be sure you write or I'll be hearing from Christine. She really is in a stew over this. When she found out Grant Nolan had an 18-year-old daughter, I got the third degree."

Silas laughed in delight at this. "She can certainly be the mother hen at times, can't she?"

"Oh, Si, if she ever heard you say that...well, I hate to even think of the tongue-lashing we would both get."

Silas agreed with him. While the men shared a laugh, the train pulled in and they stood. Luke opened his mouth to say good-bye, but Silas interrupted. "About your question, Luke. I'm not sure what I'll find in Neillsville, and it's troubling me. Will you please just pray?"

"Every day," Luke answered with assurance and, as he stood on the platform watching the train become a dot in the distance, he began right then to keep his word.

Silas, on the other hand, was not at all prayerful. Indeed, he was very tense. He attempted to empty his mind of all thought, but he failed miserably. His mind kept returning to the young woman at the end of his journey: Amy.

Silas settled back in his seat and gave in to the desire he had felt ever since Pastor Nolan spoke on Sunday, trying to picture in his mind what Amy was like now.

She had been rather coltish at 14. A bit on the awkward side, as if she were not sure what to do with all her limbs. Awkward, that is, until she sat at the piano. Silas had been mystified the first time he'd heard her play. Silas played piano and his family thought he was the best, but they'd never heard Amy Nolan. The keys somehow came alive under her small hands. And her face—it positively glowed while she played.

She was gifted, there was no doubt about that. At 28 years of age, Silas had listened to his share of pianists and he knew Amy was in a class all her own.

Silas had learned to play piano at his mother's knee—the only one of five Cameron children to show a genuine interest. Being able to play the piano that his mother had taught him on somehow helped ease the pain of losing her. Kathrine Cameron's deep love for music was transmitted to Silas through those times of practice and play.

For a short time right after her death, Silas had not played at all, out of consideration for his father. He could tell that hearing the piano pained his father greatly.

When the house was empty one afternoon, Silas sat down and played some of his favorite hymns. He had played along in a bittersweet state for nearly 30 minutes when he looked up to see his father watching him. Silas could only guess how long he'd been there.

Silas bolted from the piano bench, stumbling through an apology as he straightened the music sheets with shaky hands. His panicky movements and words came to a halt as his father started toward him.

Silently, Joseph reached for the sheets of music. He looked through them slowly before placing a single sheet back on the music rest. A quick glance told Silas it was one of his mother's favorites. "Play this one, Si. Play it the way your mother taught you." He gave Silas' shoulder a pat and moved to take a nearby chair. Before he finished the song, the entire family had gathered. One by one they entered the room, no one bothering to disguise the sound of sniffling noses. Silas barely made it through the piece.

Silas played regularly after that. The keys beneath his fingers felt like a balm applied directly to his soul.

Amy also had learned piano from her mother, but there had not been the same comfort for her. Silas had been in the Nolan home for over two weeks when, after supper one night, Grant asked Amy if she felt like playing. Silas hated the shy way she looked at him before telling her father no. He did not want to make her feel uncomfortable.

He had wished he could tell her he understood the hurt. He had been only 13 when his mother died. It had been only three weeks since Maureen Nolan's funeral, but Silas knew from experience that to Amy it felt like a year.

Standing quickly, Silas made a snap decision. He faced Grant and spoke. "I know I'm a poor substitute for Amy, but if you've no objections, I'd like to play."

Grant answered with a small smile, "Please, Silas, feel free." But Silas didn't move with Grant's consent alone. He turned to the sober young girl in the room, who was regarding him with big, surprised eyes.

"Do you have any objections, Amy?"

"No." She didn't hesitate in answering, but her voice was so low that Silas saw more than heard her answer.

At the piano, Silas played wholly from memory. Within minutes, the other occupants of the room were forgotten as he moved from one song to the next. The piano's tone was beautiful, and Silas pulled deep within himself as he played piece after piece.

He would never know exactly what brought him back to the present, but just then he looked over at Amy and she smiled at him. For an instant, Silas was so surprised he didn't respond. It was the first time this quiet girl had shown anything past an indifferent, neutral acceptance of him in her home.

When Silas finally returned the smile, Amy's grew wider. They sat there grinning at one another while Silas finished the song.

Not long afterward the three retired for the night. As Silas readied himself for bed in his small attic bedroom, he was sure the ice had broken through for Amy and him. He really did want to be her friend.

Every day for nearly three weeks Silas had worked alongside her father, working steadily even when Grant slowed down or came to a complete halt. After a week, Grant began to talk and Silas listened without comment to the man's heartache, his concern for Amy foremost in his mind.

The days the men worked and talked seemed to be a gentle push for Grant onto the road of acceptance and recovery.

Not so with Amy. She grieved silently without complaint or comment. It was at this time Silas realized how much he'd taken his siblings for granted. Amy needed a big brother to help shoulder the grief.

As Silas settled into bed, he knew he wanted to be that big brother. "Please, God," Silas prayed as he dropped off to sleep, "help Amy open up to me. Let her know that I care and understand." Remembering the smile she had given him, he fell asleep, sure that tomorrow would be different. But it would be a few more days and a ruined breakfast before the ice broke completely.

Silas was jolted out of his reverie when the conductor passed through the train and announced there would be a delay at the next stop. There were grumbles throughout the car, but Silas was just glad he'd left Baxter early.

The conductor said to feel free to get out and stretch a bit, so Silas moved out of his seat toward the door.

They were stopped in Elroy, a small town not too many miles out of Baxter. Silas quickly decided not to wander about and took a bench in the shade to watch the busy activity of the depot.

It wasn't long before the sights of the depot grew mundane and Silas' thoughts wandered back to the time he and Amy finally became friends.

Grant and Silas walked from the barn to the house. The milking was done and both men were ready for a big breakfast. They were greeted at the door not by the smell of fresh coffee and biscuits, but by the pungent odor of burned bacon and eggs.

Amy stood with the frying skillet in one hand while waving a dishcloth over the smoky mess with the other. When she saw her father, she simply said, "I'm sorry, Dad. Breakfast will be a little late this morning."

"Don't worry about it, Amy. I'll wash up and give you a hand." And that was the end of that. Amy didn't cry or offer a long excuse, just a simple apology and it was over. Silas was impressed.

The moment of friendship arrived when Silas also washed up and, stepping behind Amy, took the burned skillet from her hands. "I'll get this for you." The look of surprise on her face could only bc matched by the expression on her face when he'd asked to play the piano a few days earlier.

Silas didn't wait for a comment from Amy but simply proceeded to scrape the pan clean. Amy's surprise turned to genuine puzzlement when he did not return the skillet but put in strips of bacon and began to crack eggs into a bowl.

The three worked together in silence, Grant and Amy both sending a look in Silas' direction now and then. The meat was eaten as silently as it had been prepared. Grant and Silas were still at the table with their coffee when Amy was ready to leave for school. She kissed her father goodbye and then moved over to Silas. He smiled at her and said, "Have a good day, Amy."

"Thank you, Silas." Amy spoke these words just before bending and planting a quick kiss on his cheek. Silas turned to stare at her as she bolted for the door. Neither man spoke of it the rest of the day, but Silas noticed for the first time that Grant whistled while they went about their daily work.

A precious friendship began that day and Silas boarded the train with a feeling of contentment in his heart brought on by his reflection of that time. The friendship he and Amy shared had been special, one that no amount of time could obliterate. Each held a special place in the heart for the other.

The remainder of the trip, if uneventful, was less worrisome for Silas. By the time he arrived in Neillsville, it was raining. Silas had planned to hire a horse from the livery and ride the two-and-a-half miles out to the Nolan farm, but the rain caused him to reconsider.

Reasoning to himself there was no guarantee the rain would let up tomorrow, Silas went ahead toward the livery. He might as well get wet today as tomorrow.

It was dark and gloomy as he rode out of Neillsville, and he could feel the reluctance of the animal beneath him. Not that he blamed the poor beast. This was not fit weather for anyone. Silas only hoped, as he picked up the pace a bit, that Pastor Nolan's letter had arrived and his appearance would be expected.

6

Amy muffled a small groan as she stood up from her cramped position on the milking stool. How excited she and her father had been at the freshening of two more heifers just last month. Now, with only two more cows to go and her back screaming, Amy couldn't help wondering what they'd been so excited about. The morning milking never hurt her back like the afternoon milking did, and Amy, in her tired state, never stopped to think that the full schedule she kept between the morning and afternoon milking may have something to do with that fact.

The milking and cleanup finally completed, Amy threw her cape over her shoulders and, with head bent to watch every step, she moved carefully across the puddle-strewn yard to the house. Doctor Schaefer was scheduled to see her father sometime that night, and Amy wanted to be present.

Not until Amy was on the porch did she look up to see if Doc's carriage was in the yard. Although on this rainy night he would probably have come right into the barn, Amy peered through the rain-darkened evening for signs of him and saw none. Satisfied she had finished before he arrived, she went in to check on her father.

Grant sat back against the pillows of his bed and heard the front door open and close. He waited quietly, without calling, knowing Amy would come to check on him as soon as she was dry. The pain was only a dull ache, but the frustration was ever-present. Having to lay in bed while his daughter did his work was almost more than he could bear.

"Doc should be here anytime, Dad. How about some supper?" Amy spoke as she entered the room and sat down gently on the bed, moving carefully so as not to jar his leg.

"Let's eat after he comes. First, tell me if there is any trouble with the cows."

Amy was accustomed to this question. Even when her father had been in great pain, he asked after the cows. He went on before she could answer. "I hate to see you go out in this rain. You didn't get a chill, I hope." Amy almost laughed over the fact that he asked about the cows before checking on his daughter. He was like an overanxious mother where those cows were concerned. But considering they were the source of family income, she couldn't say as she blamed him.

"The cows are fine, including the latest milkers, who are doing great. Everything is closed up for the night, and I did not catch a chill," Amy recited quickly, hoping she had omitted nothing and that his worries would be eased, but a funny look came over his face.

"Amy, am I driving you nuts?"

Amy was so surprised by this question, she laughed outright. "Dad," she gasped, "what in the world are you talking about?"

But he did not join in her merriment, and she tried hard to pull a straight face. "When have I ever had trouble milking? If there was a problem, you would be the first to know. And the second you start to drive me crazy, you'll also be the first to know."

This brought a small smile to Grant's face and he asked, "You're sure everything is fine?"

"Positive." Amy said with a smile. "How's the leg?"

"Better, much better. It usually throbs in the night, so I'm afraid you'll have to get used to sleeping the days away for a bit longer."

"Well, as much as I'd like to see you out of that bed, I'll tell on you in a hurry if you rush things."

"I'm sure you will. You're as bossy as your mother was." They both laughed at this. Maureen Nolan had been the most *un*bossy woman on the face of the earth.

Old Doc Schaefer arrived as Amy was fixing supper. He readily agreed to stay for the meal, and the amount of stomach stretching his binders gave proof that he rarely turned down such offers.

Doc checked Grant over and was pleased to see him progressing so well. Between Amy and the doctor, Grant was able to eat at the kitchen table for the first time in nearly two weeks. Conversation was lighthearted for most of the meal and, having escaped the bed, Grant was in high spirits.

Over coffee and dessert, Doc Schaefer asked a surprising question. "Had you heard? Carltons were robbed last night."

"Robbed?" Amy was incredulous. "What in the world was there to steal?" Amy's question was valid. The Carltons had a very small farm and usually had a hard time making it from month to month.

"Well, Harold must have told one too many people he was planning on taking some of that inheritance money from Ruth's aunt for farm repairs."

"But Ruth said that money was in the bank."

"It was until yesterday and then was stolen last night."

The table was silent as Grant and Amy digested this bit of news. More coffee was served and the three talked on until it was evident Grant had overestimated his strength. The rain had not let up and so as soon as they had Grant settled back in bed, Doc took his leave.

He and Amy talked for a bit but, with the rain continuing, Amy wanted to get out and check the stock one last time before settling in for the evening.

"Amy," Grant said as she was leaving, "take the shotgun out with you." Amy's eyebrows rose in surprise at this, and for a moment she hesitated. "Please, honey, it would make me feel better."

Amy nodded silently and headed for the door. She realized that until just then she hadn't even thought of the thieves still being in the area.

The gun felt cold against Amy's side as she made her way across the yard for a final check on the animals. She tried to squelch the fear she felt as she stepped carefully around the puddles, but the desire to do double checks on the shadows was a temptation. Psalm 56:3 came to mind as she moved toward the barn: "What time I am afraid, I will trust in thee." After thinking of these words, Amy knew instant comfort.

The rain was not a hard downpour, but a steady shower. The warmth and familiar smells of the barn were an added comfort as Amy stepped within. She leaned the gun against a post while lighting the lantern.

The wind seemed to pick up as did the rain as she walked along the stalls. Amy was angry with herself for the fear she felt. She knew God was watching over her and once again claimed the verse in Psalms. Everything was in order and Amy had just blown out the lamp and picked up the gun, when the door was opened wide.

Having just ridden in the dark, Silas was a few steps into the barn before his eyes made out a lone figure pointing a gun at him. He froze and felt his heartbeat accelerate. He had wondered how he would be greeted at the Nolan farm, but this was ridiculous.

"State your business, mister, and do it quickly." The voice speaking from behind the gun was high-pitched with fear, but Silas recognized it.

"I'll state my business, Amy Nolan! You've got exactly two seconds to get that gun pointed in another direction, or I'll do it for you!" His voice was gruff with relief, and he was just a bit angry.

The gun lowered slowly. "Silas?" The voice went up still another octave.

"Silas?" Silas mimicked in a high imitation of her voice.

With that the words came pouring out as she tried to light the lamp. "Oh, Silas! Oh no, I'm so sorry! I can't believe I held a gun on you. You scared me and you see there was this robbery and well, I wasn't expecting anyone to come in." The words stopped as abruptly as they had started when the lamp was finally lit and turned high. Amy could only stare at the drenched man before her. Silas stared back. Amy watched the flash of white in his beard as a slow smile started.

"Hi." Silas' voice was soft now, and deep.

"You mean you're speaking to me?" Amy asked, her tone dry. Silas' laughter echoed in the barn, and he reached to give her a quick hug.

"I take it from your reaction, I've arrived ahead of your uncle's letter?"

"There's been no word on your coming, but I'm so glad you're here." Amy's voice was sincere and childlike all at once.

"How is your dad?"

"He's doing better, and he'll be thrilled to see you."

They stared at each other for a few more minutes, Amy feeling like she could hug him again but remembering she was not 14 anymore. Silas thought how grown up she was.

They worked together to stable Silas' horse and, as they made their way across to the house, Silas had the odd sensation he was coming home.

— ❖ —

"You would think the boss could have put this off for one night. I'm freezing."

The man to whom he spoke only grunted in reply and continued to stare out into the rain. Within ten minutes, coming from the direction of town rode a black-cloaked figure on an equally black mount. The men stood silently as the horse and rider entered the broken-down barn that had stood abandoned for years.

Without dismounting, the rider spoke. "You have the money?" The voice was husky and low, and the two men within the barn tried to make out the face of their mysterious employer. The turned-up collar of the cloak, along with the low brimmed hat, kept the rider's identity as dark as the night.

Wordlessly, bags were exchanged. A large sack was handed up to the rider and quickly concealed beneath the cloak.

Anticipating the next move, the two men caught small bags as they sailed from atop the horse.

The chink of coins as the bags landed in the outstretched hands was the only sound made as the two men watched the rider turn the mount and disappear into the wet gloom.

"Who do you suppose he is?"

"I don't have a clue, but if we start asking questions the money will stop," the other man spoke as he tucked the moneybag into his belt. "And *that* is a risk I'm not willing to take."

7

Silas lay on his back in bed. The vaulted ceiling was familiar, as were the smells and sights of his attic bedroom. The room was simply furnished with a bed, washstand, and dresser. Moonlight streamed through a small, yellow-curtained window and shone on Silas' clothes where they hung from a hook on the wall. Next to the hanging clothes was a small wooden chair. For Silas there was a strange sense of comfort in seeing everything as he remembered.

Silas had the same feeling with Grant and Amy, even though there had been changes. The three of them had taken about an hour to get reacquainted, and Silas was amazed at how welcome they had made him feel. It was as if they had never been separated.

As he lay musing, Silas remembered that Amy had said something about a robbery. He would have to ask her tomorrow. Right now he was too tired to think. He knew the morning would bring hard work—not that he had ever been afraid of work, but getting a good night's sleep was beginning to blot out all other thought.

He knew this was where God wanted him, and it gave him a feeling of contentment as he drifted off to sleep that could only be matched by that of the two people readying for sleep downstairs.

— ✤ —

Amy had never prepared for bed so slowly. Her mind kept going over and over the events of the last two hours when Silas had appeared in the barn, and then seeing her look of surprise mirrored on Grant's when Silas' large frame had filled her father's bedroom doorway.

Silas carried with him an air of confidence that brought with it a sense that all was going to be well.

37

Four years ago God had given Amy a big brother, for six weeks, in the form of Silas Cameron. Silas had come to them like an armored knight in days of old, at a time when their pain and confusion over losing their wife and mother was so great, they didn't believe their world would ever be normal and happy again.

Quiet and sensitive, Silas had offered comfort and stability in his warm, gentle way. Amy had never known a better listener. She smiled to herself as she began to brush her hair. Silas was back, and everything was going to be just fine.

— ✤ —

For the first time in over two weeks Grant's mind was not on the throbbing in his leg as he tried to fall asleep.

Silas Cameron! Who would have thought God's answer to his prayers would be Silas Cameron? Grant had never even thought of him as he had prayed and asked God to help them through this time of hurt.

But he was here, and Grant knew all was going to be well. Amy had been an angel, but Grant could see the extra work was weighing on her. She was used to the long hours and even the milking, but not the handling of the milk cans and all of her regular work besides.

Grant had also been more than a little worried about borrowing from savings to hire field help. But the crops had to be planted, and as frustrating as Grant's helplessness was it didn't change that fact.

If the crops did not go in, money from savings would be needed to buy feed for his stock. He would be forced to buy through the winter and until next years' harvest—a very unsettling thought.

"Silas can do the planting and take over the milking and hauling. I'll get back on my feet, and by the fall I'll be off my back and ready for harvest...." These were the thoughts with which Grant fell asleep.

8

Amy was halfway across the yard before she realized the barn door was partially open. Quickening her steps while avoiding mud puddles, Amy approached the barn in unbelief. Silas had actually beaten her to the milking.

Amy stood a few minutes just inside, recovering from her surprise, when a deep voice spoke from amid a row of various-colored cows. "There is no reason for you to be out here, Amy. I can take care of everything."

Amy followed the voice until she stood at Silas' side. When he raised his head, she spoke with a teasing voice, "Am I being dismissed?" Before he could answer, Amy began to laugh at his appearance. "Oh, Silas," she said between giggles, "I forgot how much you look like a bear in the mornings."

Her words so mimicked Luke's opinion of Silas' morning appearance, he had to smile. Amy returned the smile with a warm one of her own and said, "I'll have breakfast ready when you get in."

Within the hour Silas was in the kitchen bending over the washstand. After brushing his hair and beard into some semblance of order, he headed to the table that was the focal point of the Nolan kitchen.

The room was not overly large, and the table and stove took up most of the floor space. Over six feet in length and easily four feet wide, the table was space-consuming by any standard, but seemed especially so with just Silas sitting and watching Amy dish up food from the stove.

She had outdone herself this morning. Silas' eyes took in eggs, sausage, bacon, fried potatoes, biscuits, three choices of jam, oatmeal, milk, and coffee. As Amy continued to work, Silas' eyes skimmed over the room he had briefly passed through the night before. It was as he remembered.

Two small windows looked out over the front yard. The curtains were very plain white cotton, but somehow fitting in this simple room. Hooks on the wall, a washstand, stove, and small, low worktable along one wall—yes, everything was as he recalled.

When Amy joined Silas at the table, she asked him to pray. She was impressed again with the feeling that all was going to be well as Silas petitioned God on behalf of Grant Nolan. Silas asked God outright to ease Grant's pain and put him back on his feet. He prayed with such assurance that Amy felt that was exactly what God would do.

When the prayer ended, they ate in companionable silence until Silas questioned Amy about the robbery. Amy told him what they had learned from Doc and then ended with, "I plan to drive into town tomorrow. I always take time to see Aunt Bev, so I'm sure she'll give me any news we've missed out here."

"Does she ever come out here to see you?" Silas asked, although quite sure what the answer would be.

"No. Uncle Evan forbids it." Her voice was so sad that Silas wished he'd kept his question to himself.

Grant woke not long after breakfast and Silas went in to see him. The two men spent the next two hours in deep conversation. Amy moved between the bedroom and the kitchen getting her father's breakfast and then bringing coffee as the morning slipped by.

When Silas finally left the bedroom so Grant could get some more rest, he knew exactly what Grant wanted done in the next several weeks. The milking and hauling, the fields, and care for the animals—they had covered it all. Silas would also be finishing the painting of the barn and house—the very cause for Grant's bedridden condition, and not a comfortable subject.

When Silas had first brought up the matter of doing the painting, Grant had said absolutely not, the painting could wait. But Silas was undeterred and, after some coaxing and reasoning, Grant had agreed to tell what his plans had been prior to falling from the ladder.

When Silas sat down to the table for noon dinner, he was holding a list of supplies he would need from town. He and Amy discussed the list and agreed that it would be easiest if he accompanied her. They planned to leave the following morning after breakfast. They would stop on the way so Amy could ask a neighbor to check on Grant at midday and get his meal.

The remainder of the day went by with chores and small talk. Silas helped Grant to the kitchen table for supper, and the three of them talked and laughed long after the dishes were cleared and the coffeepot empty. It was a warm and special beginning to Silas' stay with the Nolans.

9

Two-and-a-half miles northwest of town nestled into the base of a rocky bluff sat the Nolan farm. It was not a farm handed down from earlier generations of Nolans, but it had been home to Amy for as long as she could remember.

Grant's father, as a very young man, had come to Neillsville to work in the logging industry there. Grant was born into this rough existence and even worked for a time in the logging trade.

But the work was dangerous and Grant, with a wife and young daughter, had wanted out. He borrowed money from the bank which was subsequently owned and operated by his wife's uncle and brother, and bought a small, ill-kept dairy farm not far from town. Grant moved his wife, Maureen, and small daughter, Amy, to the farm when Amy was 3 years old.

The barn was large, with more than enough room to house the 19 healthy cows Grant milked. His milk went daily to the Daisy Cheese Factory at the edge of town, a steady income he'd banked on for years.

The farmhouse was small and white with a high-pitched roof. A small porch led up to the front door that opened into the kitchen. Two bedrooms and a living room completed the downstairs. Simple-cut stairs in the living room went up to the bedroom in the attic.

Silas and Amy emerged from the house as a clear morning sun warmed the ground. Silas in clean, blue denim pants and a red plaid shirt walked beside Amy whose dress was a soft yellow print. She tied on a matching bonnet as the couple moved across the yard to the barn where Silas had the wagon and team waiting.

Silas watched Amy glance back at the house and broke into her thoughts. "If you're worried about your dad being alone, I could take your list for town."

Amy shook her head in rather sad resignation as she answered, "No, Silas. Dad would be upset if he thought I stayed on his account. But thanks for the offer." Amy stopped by the wagon and looked up to meet Silas' eyes. "I suppose you think I'm being rather silly, but he's so helpless in that bed. I would just feel sick if anything more happened."

Silas answered as he helped her into the wagon. "On the contrary, I would think something was wrong with you if you could leave without a backward glance. Do you trust Mrs. Brewer to check on your dad?" At Amy's nod he continued, "Then I think you should leave with a peaceful heart, knowing you've taken care of everything."

Amy was thankful for his logic, and when a quarter mile up the road they stopped at the Brewer's farm, all doubts vanished.

"Of course I'll check on your father," Mrs. Brewer assured Amy. "I'll take Sammy with me, and we'll see to his every need. You know I'm always happy to give you a hand. It's important for a woman to get out to town when she can. Lifts the spirits, I always say."

Amy smiled at this woman who, along with her husband and sons, had been such a help and encouragement since her father's accident. It was to them she had run when her father had called from the yard in agony. The bone in his leg had actually come through the skin, and his entire body had seemed to lie at an impossible angle. Amy had been unable to move Grant from his crumpled position at the bottom of the ladder. So, upon arriving at the Brewer farm, Mr. Brewer and their oldest son, Dave, raced with Amy back to the house while Sammy was sent for the doctor.

Among the three of them, they had moved Grant to his bed and were keeping him warm when the doctor arrived.

"Yes, Silas was right," Amy thought as she introduced him to Mrs. Brewer. "I completely trust my father to this woman's capable hands."

The prospect of time in town had Amy's mood high as the land leveled out and the houses of the main street came into view.

Their first stop was at the bank where Amy hoped to catch sight of her Uncle Evan. Much to her disappointment, he was out. Amy made a withdrawal while Silas returned his rented horse and saddle to the livery.

When Silas picked her up, Amy asked him to drive the team to the general store. She had her list of household supplies and Silas had Grant's list for the farm. Amy saw familiar faces everywhere as they made their way past the hat shop, a boardinghouse, saloons, and numerous lumber dealers. The sight of Amy aboard her own wagon with a strange bearded man at the reins brought many stares and a few hesitant waves.

Hesitant that is, until Silas pulled up in front of one of the general stores. Mrs. Anderson, the owner's wife, who was always on the lookout for new faces and news, nearly ran into them on the boardwalk out front.

"Well, Amy dear, you've been such a stranger lately. How is your father? We've missed you on Sundays the last few weeks. We really do hope you'll be out soon. No one can play like you do. I'm afraid you've got us all spoiled."

Amy noted with amusement that while all the comments and questions were directed to her, Mrs. Anderson's eyes rarely left Silas Cameron's handsome face.

"Well, Amy dear," Mrs. Anderson said with some reproof in her tone and a raised brow, "aren't you going to introduce me to your friend?"

A quick glance at Silas told Amy he was as amused as she was by the woman's long-winded speech, but his manners were impeccable as Amy did the honors.

"Mrs. Anderson, this is Silas Cameron, a friend of my family's from the Reedsburg area. Silas, this is Mrs. Anderson. She and her husband run the general store and post office."

Even as Silas shook the woman's hand and attempted to greet her politely, she began to speak. "Well, how nice to meet a friend of Amy's." No one missed the emphasis she put on friend.

"Tell me, Silas—I hope it's alright to call you Silas?"

"Certainly."

"Tell me, Silas, are you looking to settle in this area? Possibly planning to make your home here?"

"Well no, ma'am. Actually I'm here to help at the Nolans' while Grant gets back on his feet."

"Oh well," her voice was filled with disappointment. "I hope you have a nice stay." She looked at Amy with genuine regret in her eyes. Then with a sudden "oh goodness," Mrs. Anderson's regret was replaced by curious interest. "There's Milly Baker with her new baby. You two go on inside. Ed will see to you."

Silas stared after the once-again-talking woman until he felt Amy's hand on his arm. "Is she always like that?"

Amy laughed. "Oh yes, she's never the same twice. The only thing that stays the same is her ever-present desire to see her daughters marry. I'm afraid you crushed her by telling her you were not going to be living here for the rest of your life."

Silas kept his thoughts to himself as he entered the store, but the idea of Mrs. Anderson as a mother-in-law was a bit disconcerting. Once inside, the couple wasted no time selecting the items on their list. In short order everything was loaded and paid for and they were on their way to see Bev Randall.

10

One of Neillsville's most prominent citizens in 1888 was Evan Randall. He owned and ran the largest bank in town— a business and position he had inherited from his uncle, Dell Randall. The Randall name was one of importance and commanded respect in the town of Neillsville. The Randall men were not known for their warmth or social skills, but over the years no one could fault them for their shrewd business sense and the way they turned a profit at every hand.

Amy knew all about her uncle's business acumen, and she was not blind to the fact that he completely blamed Grant Nolan for his sister's death. He believed life on the farm was too hard and that the work had shortened her life. He was sure she would have stood stronger against the illness that claimed her if her life hadn't been so rough.

In fact, he had never approved of the marriage between his sister Maureen and Grant, even before Grant began to farm. Older than Maureen by five years and already working under his Uncle Dell at the bank, Evan's aspirations for his sister went much higher than a man who worked for one of the small logging firms in town.

The fact that 18-year-old Maureen was head over heels in love with Grant Nolan or that his Uncle Dell had given his complete approval made little difference. The whole idea was repulsive to him and he was thoroughly against his beloved sister marrying someone he felt was beneath her.

He rarely spoke to Maureen during the first 18 months of her marriage to "that logger" as Evan disdainfully put it, until Maureen presented him with a tiny blonde niece named Amy.

Evan's heart melted at the sight of the little girl, and this was the Evan Randall Amy knew. He was never too rushed

47

to talk with her. Opinions that he was cold were completely groundless in the presence of his niece.

The plain truth was, Evan Randall was willing to do anything for her. The love Amy had for her uncle was straight from her heart, and she recognized that not even his sweet wife, Bev, received the special smiles she did and this bothered her.

Bev never seemed upset with her or jealous, but to Amy it was obvious, as she was sure it was obvious to everyone else, that Evan Randall thought his niece most special—as special as his sister had been. As Amy grew older, she began to see that Evan was pouring into her all the love he hadn't been able to give to his sister in the last four years.

This special relationship between Amy and her uncle had always been a source of security and joy to her. But recently something had come up, and Amy was unsure how to deal with it. Worry invaded her peace. Amy was thinking of it even as Silas pulled the team to a stop in front of a huge white mansion.

A deep, wide porch ran along the entire front of the majestic-looking home. Thick white pillars supported the flat porch roof that gracefully fronted the second-story windows.

The tenuous thread that held the Nolan and Randall families together had been abruptly severed with Maureen's death, so Silas had never been here. He let out a low, appreciative whistle as his eyes moved over the exterior.

Amy smiled with some pride. "It's beautiful, isn't it? My mother grew up in this house. I had forgotten until this moment that you haven't seen it or met my aunt and uncle."

Silas usually took hospitality for granted, but with the little information he had on these two families, and the quiet way Amy had ridden in the seat beside him, he had to ask, "Amy, maybe it would be best if I didn't stay. I could get lunch downtown and come back for you later. It would give you a chance to have a private visit with your aunt."

The shock on Amy's face was genuine. "Silas, why would you think such a thing? Aunt Bev knows all about you, and I know she'll want to meet you. You couldn't be more welcome in this home."

Silas immediately assumed he had mistaken her pensive look in the wagon. "Honestly, Amy, I meant no offense. It'll be a pleasure to meet your family."

Amy stood and looked at Silas even after he lifted her from the wagon. Silas smiled into the light-blue eyes regarding him so intently. She seemed very vulnerable to him at that moment. It became clear that his meeting and liking her aunt and uncle must be important to her.

Silas gently placed his hands on Amy's small shoulders and his smile became very tender. "Amy, I know the relationship between your father and uncle is painful for you. I would be a liar if I said I never thought of it, because it bothers me too. But I want to meet the Randalls. I know how special they are to you, and I'm sorry my question sounded so insensitive."

After a moment Amy smiled back. "You're always so logical, Silas. I think we get along very well together."

"I think we do too. Besides," he spoke as he took her arm and led her toward the door, "*that* is what big brothers are for."

Amy continued in his light-hearted mood. "It's a nice arrangement I've got, having a part-time big brother. If we'd grown up together, you would be bossy and tease me all the time. This way if you step out of line, I won't feed you."

"Ah, but you're forgetting, I can cook!"

"That does pose a problem. If I can't get to you through your stomach, I'll have to come up with something else to keep you in shape."

They shared a final teasing smile before Silas reached up to knock at the front door. It was by mutual, unspoken consent that they waited in silence for the door to open.

11

"Hello, Perkins. Is my aunt home?" After some moments the front door had opened and Amy was addressing her question to an elderly gentleman with a full head of gray hair and a stately manner about him that he wore like a cloak.

"Of couse, Miss Amy." The man nodded, his face expressionless. The couple moved into the foyer as Perkins stepped aside and opened the door wide. "I'll tell Mrs. Randall you're here." His manner was so formal that it was almost comical.

After he moved away, Amy looked at Silas. She had to stifle a giggle with her hand as she watched his brows raise and eyes twinkle. Knowing her laughter would only start his own, Silas turned away from her to survey his surroundings.

Dual staircases rose from the foyer to the second floor in a straight, formal fashion. To the right of the foyer was a small parlor with large windows overlooking the porch. In one corner stood a small fireplace.

Another room—appearing to be a library—branched off the parlor, but Silas did not move to investigate. His eyes swung to the left of the foyer and took in a large living room running almost the full length of the house.

This room, as well as the foyer sported huge windows, some accented with colored or ornately etched glass. The living room overlooked the porch and was full of beautiful furniture. Several doors exited off this room, and Silas felt an urge to explore. He glanced at Amy to find her watching him.

"Were you hoping I'd be impressed?" Silas' expression was knowing.

"Are you?" Amy's grin was downright cheeky.

"What if I said no?" Silas asked with an elaborate shrug.

"I'd say you were a poor liar, Si Cameron."

"You'd be right," Silas said with a laugh.

"Amy," a deep, almost-masculine voice called from the living room. Amy turned and rushed into the arms of a tall, reed-slim woman.

Silas watched as the two shared a long hug. When at last they separated, Bev Randall held Amy at arm's length. The unfeigned concern Silas saw written on her face endeared her to him immediately. "How is Grant?"

"A little better every day, but he's been in so much pain," Amy answered in a trembling whisper, and Silas knew without seeing her face that she was fighting tears. Her aunt knew also and pulled her once again into a firm embrace.

"I wanted to come, but . . . well . . ." The words died in the older woman's throat as Amy nodded her head in silence. Once again the two hugged, this time in unspoken understanding.

Silas suddenly found himself the center of attention. Both women had turned to him and Silas stood quietly, studying Amy's aunt as intently as she was studying him.

The face before him was thin, cheeks nearly sunken. Something about her mouth led Silas to believe she didn't smile often. Her eyes were shrewd but not unkind, nor did they waver from his own as she began to speak in an almost-stern tone of voice.

"From Amy's description, you can't be anyone other than Silas Cameron." She paused, and the young people in the room were almost tense as they waited for her to continue. But when she did, there was kindness in her rather gravelly voice. "I must admit that when Amy told me about you four years ago, I believed it could only be a 14-year-old's imagination that could create such size. But I was wrong," she said as she stepped forward with her hand outstretched. "You *are* big."

"It's a pleasure to meet you, Mrs. Randall."

"Please call me Bev and allow me to thank you for coming to help Grant and Amy."

"Aunt Bev," Amy broke in, "how did you know Silas was here to help us?"

"Oh, that's easy. Two nights ago a large, bearded man arrived by train when the skies were dumping rain on Neillsville. He rented a horse and headed in the direction of the Nolan farm." Bev smiled at Amy, who was beginning to catch on, and continued her story to a still-confused Silas. "You see, Silas, there isn't much in this town that goes on without my knowledge. Remembering Amy's description of you and the direction you headed that night along with finding you in my front room . . . well, you see it didn't take a detective."

The three laughed at this logical explanation for Bev's nosiness, but Amy sobered quickly upon remembering something.

"Aunt Bev, had you heard about the robbery at the Carlton farm?"

Bev nodded silently, and Silas and Amy watched a pained, troubled expression cross over her features. She opened her mouth to speak, but just then the front door burst open and in strode Evan Randall.

12

Silas spooned soup into his mouth from the most beautiful china bowl he had ever seen. The spoon in his hand was heavy with a large, ornate "R" engraved on the handle. It was obvious even to the most casual observer that everything in the Randall dining room, and probably the entire house, was of high quality and cost.

As he continued to eat, Silas watched Evan Randall converse with his niece. Silas tried to look at Amy, but she was partially hidden by a vase of fresh flowers sitting on the table between them.

Silas found it odd that Evan made no attempt to include him or his wife in the conversation. Still, Silas continued to study the man.

He was slim like his wife and a few inches taller. His hair was a medium shade of brown but his thin mustache and short, pointed beard were nearly black. Silas studied the man's eyes. They were unsmiling eyes—even when the corners of Evan's mouth had turned up, his eyes had stayed flat, almost expressionless. Silas remembered the way they had skimmed over him earlier when they were introduced. Silas had the distinct impression he'd been assessed and found wanting.

Silas' thoughts were interrupted when the soup bowls were removed. He met Amy's blue eyes just over the top of a red rose when the butler announced the serving of roast duck. Those eyes twinkled at him before Amy turned to answer a question posed by her uncle.

The meal progressed, and by the time dessert arrived Silas was a bit antsy. He was not used to taking so much time over a midday meal, and especially when he had not been allowed more than two sentences' worth of conversation.

Amy also must have been aware of the time. Not more than ten minutes passed after the end of the meal when she said they had to be leaving. She hugged her aunt good-bye and promised to return soon. Silas stayed in the house a moment longer to add his thanks to Bev Randall as Evan walked Amy to the wagon. Once outside, he caught part of their conversation as he approached.

"Please, Amy, don't reject the idea out of hand. You'll always be welcome in this home. If you don't feel good about leaving your father in someone else's care, then plan to come when he's back on his feet."

Amy opened her mouth to speak, but Evan held up his hand to forestall her. "Don't give me an answer now. Just think on it and know the offer I made before your father's accident still stands."

"Alright, Uncle Evan, I'll talk to you later." Amy's voice sounded almost sad.

Silas had boarded the wagon and was surprised when Evan reached across Amy to shake his hand. His smile was almost warm. His words were even more surprising. "I'm glad you're here, Silas. I hope with your help Amy's father will be up and about soon." He didn't wait for a reply but turned and walked back to the house.

Silas sat for moment and stared at the woman beside him. When she did not look at him, but sat staring somewhere beyond the horse's ears, he spoke. "I don't suppose you'd care to tell me what that was all about?" He watched Amy frown and bite her lower lip, telling him she'd heard his question, but she made no move to answer.

Just as silently, Silas urged the team forward. Amy still had not spoken at the edge of town and Silas left her to her thoughts even though his were racing. He had not liked the bit of conversation he'd heard or the unexpected words directed to him from the town banker. Something told him Evan Randall never acted unselfishly. Silas shook his head slightly over his judgmental attitude. The last thing Evan Randall needed was Silas' condemnation. What he really needed was prayer, and Silas was suddenly thankful for Amy's silence as he began to pray silently.

Amy, sitting so quietly on her side of the wagon, was praying also. Not just praying, but begging God for wisdom in this impossible situation that was bound to bring pain to someone she loved.

A few weeks before her father's accident, Evan had approached her about coming to live in town with him and Bev. Amy had been so surprised that she had not known what to say. She had rarely seen her uncle so excited. "You have no social life when you live so far out of town. Bev and I have more space in this house than we know what to do with. I know you would never make this move without talking to your father. But I'll say this much, Amy," and here his voice grew very stern, "if your father really loves you he won't stand in the way of your happiness."

Amy had been dumfounded by his words. She had never expected to receive such an invitation from her uncle, and she wondered where in the world he got the idea she was unhappy on the farm. Amy was still reeling from shock when her uncle spoke his first insensitive words to her. "I don't have to remind you, Amy, that Debra Wheeler is a town girl. Now I think Thomas Blane is a fool to give you up and obviously not good enough for you, but the truth is that the most eligible men are from town and they would naturally want wives from town."

Had Amy not been so stunned by his words, she would have burst into tears. She was well on her way to getting over Thomas. In fact, she was doing so well she wondered if indeed it had been love she felt for him. But these words coming so cruelly from her adored uncle, that somehow her being from the farm had made her not good enough, were almost more than she could bear. Even now they caused a sharp pain in the region of her heart. It didn't help that Amy thought Debra Wheeler very beautiful and her pride had suffered a severe blow at being tossed over for one of the most attractive girls in Neillsville.

Suddenly she wanted to talk it over with Silas. But after the way she had treated him in front of her uncle's house, she wasn't sure he was speaking to her.

"Silas, are you angry with me?"

"No, should I be?"

"Yes."

"How do you figure?"

"Well, you asked me a question in town and I wouldn't even look at you."

"That's true. But did you stop to think that I asked you a question that was none of my business?"

Amy shifted on the seat to look at Silas and he pulled the team to a halt. They were still about a half mile from the house.

"Oh Silas, I wasn't offended by your question—never think that, but I'm in a terrible mess and I really need someone to talk to and it can't be my dad. If he ever found out, he'd be just crushed."

"Found out about what?" Silas asked, his eyes leveled on her face. Had she not said a word he would have known something or someone was playing havoc with her heart. For an instant he thought it might be the man she had been engaged to and wondered why this idea bothered him so much.

Amy was unaware that her face was a mask of confusion and grief as she answered. "Before Dad's accident, Uncle Evan asked me to come and live with him and Aunt Bev. Today he assured me the offer still stands."

Amy spoke the words quietly, and Silas understood almost instantly the dilemma she was in. She had long been an envoy of peace amid these two families, and now she found herself between the kettle and the coals. No matter what her choice, someone she loved was going to be hurt.

13

Grant was starved for news from town and fired many questions at Silas and Amy during supper, much to the relief of both. Time had not allowed them to sit long on the road, and they were still both in deep thought over their unfinished conversation.

"Amy," Silas had said, "I don't have answers for you right now. I need to think and pray before I can advise you, and I'm not even sure I should do that. You may need to work this out for yourself. But I'm glad you told me and when you want to talk, you know I'm here." Amy had thanked him. The regret and concern she had seen in his eyes had somehow given her a small measure of peace. She didn't feel quite so alone in her pain.

Amy had just finished the dishes when Grant called her to his room. Silas had helped him into bed after supper, then he went out for a final check on the cows. Grant asked Amy to play for a while, and Silas found her seated at the piano and playing softly when he returned.

Moving quietly, Silas settled onto the couch and let the music flow over him. Amy was in profile to him as she played, and Silas watched with the eye of a fellow musician. As always, her style and grace were beyond compare. Her hands moved with confidence as she played from memory. Silas recognized the music, noticing she went from hymns to a more difficult piece that had a soothing, almost haunting melody. His head fell back to rest on the couch and, as his eyes slid closed, he began to reflect on the day.

The Randalls wanted Amy to come and live with them— what a mess! The conversation Silas had overheard at the wagon now made complete sense. Judging from the words Evan had directed at Silas, he seemed very confident Amy would come as soon as Grant was on his feet. Silas had to admit to himself, his first reaction to the idea was negative, but who was he to judge? Maybe God wanted Amy living in town.

Amy, as far as he could see, had been working hard all her life to balance her affection between her father and uncle—a position she had not asked for but one which had been thrust upon her at birth. Judging from the relationships Amy had with both men, it was obvious she was doing an excellent job. Silas felt a bit of anger that she should now be forced into making this kind of a decision. Possibly some of the anger could better be termed frustration at having no advice to give this young woman. She held a special place in his heart, as a younger sister would. His feelings must have shown on his face because he opened his eyes when the music stopped to find Amy watching him. "The music is supposed to relax you, Si, not make you frown." She smiled at him as she spoke, but her eyes were questioning.

"It wasn't the music, Amy, I can assure you. Nothing has changed in four years; you still play like an angel."

"Just exactly how many angels have you heard play?" Amy's voice was a bit mocking.

Silas gave her a stern look. "I can see there are other things that haven't changed in four years; we've talked about this before. When someone compliments your playing, you thank them—not belittle your work with some light remark."

"But Silas, that's just it, it's not work. My playing has always come so easily that I feel guilty accepting compliments."

"It's still a gift from God, and to make light of it is wrong." The two sat regarding each other in stubborn silence for some moments. Amy spoke first.

"Were you frowning over what I told you in the wagon?" Amy was sure her dad was asleep, so she did not drop her voice.

Silas' voice was serious as he answered. "It hasn't been

far from my thoughts since you told me. Would you like to talk about it?"

Gone was the big brother who scolded her for a flip response to his compliment. In fact, Silas' voice was so tender that Amy nearly cried. She spoke slowly and Silas listened without interruption.

"A few weeks before my dad's fall, Uncle Evan approached me about coming into town to live with them. Somehow he has the impression I'm unhappy out here on the farm. Nothing could be further from the truth." She paused, but Silas kept quiet.

"Silas, had you heard I'd been engaged?" At his nod she continued. "The boy I was engaged to is from town and well, Uncle Evan felt I would meet someone else if I lived there. I've so wanted to talk with my dad, but I'm afraid he'll think I'm staying here out of some sort of obligation and it wouldn't be the truth. I don't want to move into town, but I have no idea how to tell my uncle without hurting him or making him think Dad is forcing me to stay.

"I know my uncle never meant to be mean, but he said the most eligible boys were from town and they would naturally want a wife from town. Debra Wheeler lives in town. She's Thomas Blane's new fiancée, and Uncle Evan thinks if I had been from town Thomas would not have broken up with me. I didn't tell my uncle that I plan to never marry, but I couldn't help but feel a little hurt when he implied I wasn't good enough. I also know my uncle has never accepted Christ, and I'm afraid that if the bond between us is broken, he'll never come to know the Lord."

Even in the light of this man's need for salvation, Silas was working hard at keeping a normal expression on his face as rage boiled within him. How dare her uncle make Amy feel as though she were not good enough! Thomas Blane was a fool and obviously didn't deserve her. Silas would have laughed if he'd known how closely his thoughts echoed those of Evan Randall, a man he was having more and more trouble liking all the time.

"I know you can't tell me what to do, but thank you for listening, Silas."

Silas' heart nearly broke at the forlorn look on her face. "You're right, sweetheart, I can't tell you what to do. But I will say this: I think you're doing your father a great injustice. Part of the hurt you're feeling is because you want to talk to him. I know he'll listen and help you, and you know it too. Even with a broken leg he's still the father who loves you with all his heart. He'll not let you down."

Amy sat and stared at Silas as the truth of his words came through to her. How many times had she asked God for help while possibly missing how close it had been all the time? "Thank you, Silas." Amy spoke the words softly and moved to her bedroom. Silas blew out the lanterns and headed for his own room.

Grant lay quietly in his bed listening as Silas climbed the stairs to the attic. He stared at the ceiling, feeling old beyond his years and helpless. He wanted to pray but didn't even know where to begin. After all he'd overheard tonight from the living room, the pain in his heart overpowered the pain in his leg. He felt a single tear slide down his temple, his heart crying out to God as it had so many times past, "Please God, let Your will for Amy be as special as she is."

— ✛ —

"You got the note?"

"I got it." The voice answering was sharp with anxiety.

"What's it say? We got another job to do?"

"Patience man, this barn's been standing alone for years. A light burning in here and we're as good as found out."

The testy man's companion peered out into the ebony night. There didn't appear to be anyone about, but one couldn't be too careful. Suddenly the attention of both men was drawn upward by the sound of fluttering wings—bats, no doubt. Each man reacted in his own way—one suppressed a shiver, the other pulled his hat a bit closer about his ears, and whispered, "Well, if we can't read it here, let's get back to town." The man was not about to admit his fear, but he nearly sagged with relief when his partner moved toward the horses.

As always the two were plagued by the identity of their employer, or rather the lack thereof. When at first their services had been employed, the jobs were nondescript and, even though the margin was narrow, within the confines of the law. But all this had changed a number of weeks back when they were asked to rob a farmhouse. The amount taken was very small, but it became obvious that they were being tested when the next farm robbery had yielded a substantially larger amount.

Even as the men climbed stairs at the back of the largest saloon in town and entered their room, each harbored a small hope within his breast that this note would give some clue as to the identity of the mysterious, darkly-cloaked figure with whom they were doing business.

14

The letter began "Dear Silas" and it was from his grandmother. She wrote of herself and the family, along with
asking many questions as to the welfare of the Nolan household. Silas had had precious few moments with his Grandma
Em in the last month, what with his trip to Chicago and
then leaving almost immediately for Neillsville. He missed
her more than he thought possible. The letter was the next
best thing to talking with her, but it made him feel the void
of her missing presence all the more.

Unbidden, the fact came to Silas' mind that his grandmother was not getting any younger. He couldn't imagine
life without her, and he immediately pushed the thought
aside. She was with them now and he could see no reason
to torture himself with images of a future without her.

An unfamiliar man's voice drifted up through Silas' open
bedroom door to interrupt his musing. He listened for a
moment from his place on the bed and caught sounds of
Amy's voice before setting his letter aside and descending
the stairs to appease his curiosity.

"Oh Silas, I'm glad you came down," Amy spoke the
minute she spotted him. "This is Doc Schaefer. He's here to
check on Dad."

The men shook hands and exchanged pleasantries. Both
Silas and Amy watched as the doctor moved into Grant's
bedroom with easy familiarity, shutting the door behind
him. Amy headed back into the kitchen and Silas went
outside.

The weather was warm, surprisingly so for this early in
the year, but the ground was still too wet to even start
thinking about the crops. Silas' mind turned to the painting
of the house.

Grant must have worked quickly because the front and
sides of the house were done, leaving just the back and the

trim. Standing at the back of the house, Silas could see where Grant had started to paint at the apex of the gabled roof. His eye measured the distance from the spot near the roof to the ground. No wonder Grant was in pain. Silas winced at the thought of Grant's fall.

"When do you plan to start?" Amy spoke as she came around the corner of the house.

"Monday morning, pending the weather."

Amy nodded and looked to the small section her father had already painted, far above the ground. She didn't say anything to Silas but she was determined: Come Monday she would be out here holding the ladder when he climbed it.

The couple began moving toward the front of the house. "I've asked Doc to stay for supper, it's nearly ready."

"I thought I smelled pie," Silas said with a pleased grin.

"That you did—last year's peaches." Silas held the door for Amy and, as they entered the house, the aromas that assailed Silas told him Amy had been hard at work.

Doc Schaefer was an easy man to talk with or rather to listen to. He knew everyone within miles and loved to give the latest news to any willing ear. Silas learned that Carrie Nelson had just given birth to a large, healthy girl and that he suspected Maria Southern was carrying twins.

The doctor's diagnosis on Grant had been a little less than encouraging. The healing process was slow and Grant would be off his feet for an indefinite period of time. Grant had not joined them at the supper table this night, and Silas strongly suspected his spirits were low. Both he and Amy had been in to check on him before retiring for the night and, even though Grant was talkative, Silas knew he was discouraged over his bedridden state.

Amy went to bed with much the same thought as Silas. She reached for the Bible she kept on the table by her bed and turned to the Book of Isaiah. In the fifty-fifth chapter, verses eight and nine she read, "For my thoughts are not your thoughts, neither are your ways my ways, saith the

Lord. For as the heavens are higher than the earth, so are my ways higher than your ways, and my thoughts than your thoughts." Reading these words helped restore some of Amy's peace and calm her questions about why so many painful things had entered their lives.

Suddenly Amy remembered something. She jumped out of bed to look for a poem she had written after her mother died. It was in the bottom of the chest which sat at the foot of her bed. After reading it over again, Amy thought of how good it would sound put to music.

Amy got back into bed with a purpose in her heart. She would try not to dwell on her dad's accident or on the answer she must give to her uncle and she would give special attention to putting some notes to the words of her poem.

When Amy finally did drift off to sleep, it was with a more peaceful heart and with joy that tomorrow was Sunday, a day set aside for fellowship and learning about her Lord.

15

Silas stood fingering his beard before the mirror that hung over his washstand. The words ending his grandmother's letter came back to him: "You are such a peaceful, consistent part of our lives, Silas. You never seem to change as the years go on, and sometimes I think this is what makes you so special."

He knew very well that his grandmother had meant this in only the kindest terms, but somehow the words bothered him. Silas did not believe for a moment that a man's physical appearance altered his personality—to which he was sure his Grandma Em was referring, but somehow he had this tremendous urge to change something about his looks.

He glanced down at the razor near his hand, still a little bemused at what might have compelled him to bring it along. It had been years since he'd used it. Once more he looked up into the mirror. "I'll do it," he thought. And having made up his mind, it was as good as done.

— ✛ —

Amy closed the door to her father's room. He had told her the night before that he planned to sleep late and not to worry about breakfast. He'd assured her he could wait until they got home from church to eat. But when breakfast was on the stove, Amy decided to check on him anyhow. Just as he'd predicted, he was sound asleep.

Amy was just turning away from the stove when Silas entered the kitchen. At least she thought it was Silas. The bowl of oatmeal dropped from her hands and landed hard on the table.

Silas stood completely still and watched Amy move toward him as though she were in a trance. Her beautiful blue eyes were wide as she surveyed his new face. His beard was gone. His upper lip still sported a full, dark mustache, but his beard was completely gone. Amy had always thought Silas nice-looking, but suddenly those words were a gross understatement. His jaw was strong and his chin had a tiny cleft in it. His cheeks were leaner than you would have expected to find under all that hair. Somehow the absence of his beard made his eyes stand out, and Amy noticed for the first time how blue they were. The skin of his lower face was several shades lighter than his upper cheeks and forehead, but it didn't detract from his looks. One word came quickly to mind: beautiful.

Amy was unaware that she had spoken the word aloud until Silas smiled so wide the cleft in his chin disappeared. Amy blushed to her hairline. Silas, on the other hand, was pleased beyond words.

Amy turned away in confusion, realizing that until that moment she had never looked at Silas as being anything more than a big brother. Seeing him like this, as a woman sees an attractive man, was a bit disconcerting. Suddenly she felt rather childish and wondered if maybe this was the way Thomas had perceived her, as a little girl.

"Do I really look okay, Amy?"

Amy immediately picked up the hesitancy in his voice and turned to find she was right. This big, self-assured man was in need of a little encouragement. Amy doubted that Silas knew his insecurity was written all over his face. Suddenly he was her big brother again, and Amy answered with sincerity. "You look great, Silas. I've just never noticed what pretty eyes you have." She grinned mischievously before she went on. "The girls at church will be begging for introductions. And Mrs. Anderson, before she recognizes you, will be sure I've got another suitor for her girls."

Silas touched his bare face. "I wonder if I could stick the hair back on."

Amy laughed at his chagrined tone and gave him no

mercy. "Come now, Silas, you might find one of the Anderson girls very nice."

"It isn't the girls I object to. It's the idea of Mrs. Anderson as a mother-in-law that has me doubting."

Amy laughed again, but it sounded hollow to her own ears. She couldn't understand the funny feeling coming over her at the thought of Silas interested in one of the girls at church. It was still on her mind when they pulled out of the yard in the buggy.

Amy would have been surprised to know that Silas' thoughts were along the same vein. What was it that caused a man to become more attracted to one woman than another? His brother Luke had known the women at church for years, and yet by his own admission he had had to fight his attraction for Christine almost from the moment he laid eyes on her. Had she been a Christian when they'd first met, Luke would no doubt have carried her off and married her within the first week. Silas missed them terribly, especially little Josh, but it was almost a relief to be away for a spell. Luke and Christine's marriage was a warm and loving one, and even though they never made Silas uncomfortable with their shows of affection, they did make him long for a wife and child of his own.

Suddenly Silas' thoughts turned to Amy. How was it for her after planning to be married, expecting a home of her own, with a husband at her side, only to have those plans dashed in an instant?

April Nolan, Amy's aunt who lived in Baxter, knew Silas cared deeply for Grant and Amy. After Amy had written to her about the change in her wedding plans, April had talked with Silas. He was sure Amy was unaware that her aunt had shared with him.

Maybe it was because Silas had met Amy as a vulnerable 14-year-old girl who had just lost her mother, but he knew he was more than a little protective of her. The idea of seeing her hurt caused him deep pain. He worried a bit over what his reaction would be if he were to meet Thomas Blane.

Silas was so deep in his own thoughts and prayer he did not notice Amy's own silence. In fact, he was still praying as they pulled into the churchyard.

16

Silas and Amy spent the first few minutes at the church reacquainting Silas with members of the church family. Many of the faces were familiar, giving Silas a warm sense of belonging.

Amy's prediction had been correct. Mrs. Anderson bore down upon them with surprising speed, dragging two very shy-looking daughters in her wake. Even though Silas must have been a lost cause in Mrs. Anderson's eyes, he was introduced to Brenda and Clare. They were indeed shy, and Silas felt a little sorry for the awkward situation in which their mother had put them.

With the introduction over, Silas turned to see if Amy was ready to go only to find her studying him intently.

"Did you change your mind about my looks without a beard?" Amy didn't answer his teasing question, but continued to stare at him for a few moments, completely unaware of her scrutiny. "Amy, is something wrong?"

"Silas, why aren't you married?"

"What?" Silas bent low over Amy to lessen the difference in their heights; he was sure he had misunderstood her. "What did you say?"

"I asked why you have never married, but I'm sorry I did. It's none of my business." Amy could feel the warmth in her cheeks as Silas looked at her in confusion. What was the matter with her? She was never uncomfortable with Silas and not at all used to making a fool of herself. Amy watched as Silas opened his mouth to speak, but the church bell began to ring and Amy was sure the relief she saw on Silas' face was just as evident on her own.

Silas sat in the second bench as Amy moved a few feet up to the piano. Her movements were sure and graceful, but to Silas she looked preoccupied. Whatever had prompted her question to him regarding his marital status? Silas wanted to mull the thought over, but the service was starting and he tried to shift his mind to the present.

Silas watched as Pastor Johnson stepped behind the small pulpit at the front of the church. The man was small, petite in height and frame. But he had an air of authority about him, and his sermons were doctrinally sound. As much as Silas enjoyed his preaching, he had a feeling that today his mind would be elsewhere. With effort he pulled his mind away from Amy as the pastor led the small congregation in a few songs. The pastor then directed everyone to turn to Psalm 121 and to follow along as he read.

> I will lift up mine eyes unto the hills, from whence cometh my help. My help cometh from the Lord, who made heaven and earth. He will not suffer thy foot to be moved; he that keepeth thee will not slumber. Behold, he that keepeth Israel shall neither slumber nor sleep. The Lord is thy keeper; the Lord is thy shade upon thy right hand. The sun shall not smite thee by day, nor the moon by night. The Lord shall preserve thee from all evil; he shall preserve thy soul. The Lord shall preserve thy going out and thy coming in from this time forth, and even for evermore.

They sang two more songs and then were launched into the sermon. Snatches of the message from 1 John came through to Silas, but for the most part he was miles away. He glanced at Amy often and noticed she didn't even have her Bible open. When Amy rose from his side to play the closing hymn, Silas was appalled. What was the matter with him that he could not even take time from his own thoughts to hear God's Word preached?

For the most part, Silas and Amy were quiet on the ride back to the farm. Amy's mind kept returning to the few words she had with Silas before going into the church. Her embarrassment kept her quiet not only for the ride home but for most of the day.

Sunday was usually spent relaxing, so when Grant was settled back in his bed after the noon meal Amy went off to her room for the rest of the afternoon.

Silas spent the day in his room also. He prayed and read his Bible for over two hours. For some reason his prayers were very concentrated on Amy, and by the time supper rolled around he couldn't even think of her without feeling tears at the back of his eyes.

The day passed so quietly that Silas couldn't help wondering what Monday and the new week would bring.

"Amy, you don't have to do this." Silas spoke the words for the third time, but the girl on the ground stood mute, holding the ladder in firm determination. Silas tried one more time, but she wouldn't even look up at him.

He sighed in exasperation. They had argued over breakfast, they had argued while milking, and then again as Silas climbed the ladder. Or rather, Silas had argued—Amy had just listened in stubborn silence after announcing that morning that she planned to hold the ladder while he painted.

Silas started back down the ladder. Amy moved aside as he neared the bottom. He stood frowning at her, and Amy returned his look without apology. Silas was tempted to order her into the house, but he knew she wouldn't go. It would also hurt her feelings, and that was something he would not do. With this thought in mind, his words to her were kind.

"Amy, I'm not going to fall."

"That's right, you're not." The firmness of her statement would have been more believable if her lower lip had not trembled.

Something inside of Silas melted as he witnessed her fear and vulnerability. He grabbed her into his arms and gave her a fierce hug. When he set her from him, the hands holding her upper arms were tight. "Amy, I understand your fear, but I don't believe God is going to let me fall from the ladder. Your dad and I have talked. Even if you had been out here that day, you could not have stopped his fall. In fact, from what Grant described, he would have fallen on top of you had you been standing here."

Amy followed his finger as he pointed to the foot of the ladder. "Amy, you're going to have to trust God in this even though it frightens you. If it makes you feel better to hold the ladder, that's fine. But God alone has control over this."

Silas' arms dropped to his side, and Amy turned to look out over the surrounding landscape. With the way she was chewing on her lower lip, Silas was sure she wasn't seeing the land at all.

Silas figured Amy must have come to some peace because she turned to Silas after a few minutes and said, "I'll be out to check on how you're coming a little later."

Once in the kitchen, Amy stood and tried to calm the pounding of her heart. Silas was right—she could do nothing outside. It did feel better to hold the ladder, but Amy knew if she did that she would be trusting in herself and not God to keep Silas safe.

Almost of their own volition, Amy's feet moved toward her father's bedroom.

Grant was awake and looking almost as though he had been waiting for her. The curtain moved slightly against the window, and Amy instantly knew he had been. With the window open slightly, he had heard her entire conversation with Silas.

Grant patted the edge of the bed and Amy settled herself next to him. "Silas is right," he said without preamble. "God sent him to us in our time of need and I trust that God will take care of him. When he first asked me about finishing the painting I was against it, but I realized this was pride. I've had to face the fact that right now I can't climb that ladder and may never be able to again. Well, I wasn't about to let you finish the painting, so you can see I didn't have many options. Amy, your fear is understandable, but everything is going to be fine. God will take care of Silas."

Grant stared at Amy as she studied the carpet in silence. She was a young replica of Maureen. In fact, they were so much alike he even knew what she was thinking. Her silence meant she was still pondering over the situation and praying it out—so like Maureen.

Maureen. Even now a pain went through his chest. His precious Maureen—oh, how he missed her. How proud she would have been of Amy, grown into a beautiful, godly young woman.

Suddenly, almost desperately, Grant wanted Amy to know the kind of love he and Maureen had shared.

What was the matter with Thomas Blane? For him to have Amy's love and reject it was beyond comprehension. Would Amy ever give her love again?

Movement at the back of the house drew his attention, but Amy didn't change positions. Silas Cameron. A smile broke across Grant's features. For the first time Grant was very glad Thomas had broken off with Amy. He tried to slow his mind down, but it didn't work. Silas was the perfect man for . . .

"Dad, are you alright?"

Grant started and moved to see Amy looking at him with concern. "I'm fine, honey. I was just listening to Silas bump around out there and thinking." He reached over to pat his daughter's hand, and Amy looked relieved.

Amy stood. "I think I'll head out and see how he's doing."

Grant's voice stopped her at the door. "Amy, if you want to talk about anything, you know I'm here."

Amy saw the look of tender concern on her father's face and wondered exactly what had brought that on, but she simply thanked him and went out.

18

Silas stood over the basin in the kitchen and scrubbed at the paint on his right hand with a small brush. It felt as though he were removing more skin than paint. He figured he could take more time tomorrow and use some turpentine, so he put the brush down and finished washing up for supper.

Silas had already helped Grant to the table, and he and Amy were waiting patiently for Silas to sit down. Grant's spirits, which were already high, soared when Silas told him he had finished the back of the house and would concentrate on the trim the rest of the week.

They talked about the planting which could be started next week if the good weather held. Grant could see that Silas was starving, so he took pity on him and held his conversation for dessert.

Silas was on his second piece of cake when Grant said, "I'd like you to head into town this week, no later than Thursday. There are a few things you'll need for next week. Even if we get rained out of our plans, I'll feel better when we have what's on that list."

"That's fine. Amy, do you need anything from town?"

"Yes, about six items if you think you'll have time."

"I'm sure I will." He smiled and Amy smiled back. As the day progressed, the two of them seemed to be back on old terms—warm, friendly, and a bit teasing.

After Silas thanked Amy for the meal and complimented her cooking, he turned to Grant. "Grant, where would you like to be?" Silas asked the older man, able to tell he was not at all taxed from his time at the supper table as he usually was.

"I thought you'd never ask," Grant said with a twinkle in his eye. "I'd like to go into the living room and listen to my daughter play the piano."

"Well, do I have anything to say about this?" Amy said with a teasing tone. She, too, could see that her father was in fine form this evening.

"No, you don't. You just do as you're told or I'll see you out to the woodshed."

"But Dad," Amy said with a laugh, "we don't have a woodshed."

"I know, but we did when I was a kid and that threat always worked on me."

— ✤ —

Silas wondered as he settled back on the couch if he could ever grow tired of hearing Amy play. Not likely, he was sure.

The window near the piano was open, and Silas watched as the breeze lifted a strand of her golden blonde hair. With the lanterns turned high, her hair shone with health and cleanliness.

As he continued to watch her, he remembered how good she had smelled as he'd passed her in the kitchen—like spring flowers and fresh air.

Amy looked up then and smiled at her dad and then Silas. Silas' breath caught in his throat at her beauty. Even as special as she had been as a child, Silas would never have dreamed she would grow into such a beautiful young woman. Talented, loving, giving, godly—really all the things a man would want in the woman he lov...

Between one heartbeat and the next, Silas Cameron fell head over heels in love with Amy Nolan. Silas sat frozen as his heart thundered painfully in his chest. "I'm in love with her!" he thought in wonder. Silas, having thought of himself as just a big brother, a friend, and a confidant, sat looking at Amy in stunned disbelief.

He realized it had been coming for a while. He had labeled it protectiveness and the special way a brother felt for his little sister, but it was love.

Now he knew why he could listen to her playing for-ever—because he wanted to be *with* her forever. He wanted her for his wife.

This joyful realization lasted only seconds. Amy thought of him as a big brother. At one time, this was special beyond words, but a big brother was the very last thing he wanted to be to Amy right now.

Despair quickly set in as Silas remembered Amy had said she planned to never marry. Silas looked quickly away from Amy. He was afraid she would glance over and see in his eyes all he was feeling.

Silas' heart nearly stopped as he averted his eyes from Amy only to have them lock with Grant's. Grant's look was one of compassion and understanding. *He knows*, Silas realized. *He knew even before I did.*

Amy ended the number just then and Grant quickly spoke up. "I think I'm ready to turn in now, Amy. Thank you, honey, you played beautifully."

The two men went alone to Grant's room and Silas saw Grant settled in for the night. Silas turned to leave, but Grant caught his arm. Silas had been avoiding the older man's eyes. He wanted desperately to be alone with his newfound feelings. But with Grant's hand holding him, he had little choice.

Grant said not a word as Silas' eyes met his. He held the young man with his eyes as well as his hand for a long moment. Whatever he had been searching for in Silas' face he must have found, for he slowly nodded his head in silent approval and bid Silas good-night.

Silas' good-night to Amy was hasty. He had to escape to his room. He wasn't the least bit tired, but the need to be alone was overpowering. It was long into the night before he slept.

19

"Silas, do you miss your mom?"

"Very much."

Amy's mind was four years back in time. Silas had been scheduled to leave for home in two days. They were talking up on the bluff behind her house, seated beneath the big oaks. The spot was Amy's favorite thinking place.

"Do you think about her all the time?"

"Not so much now, but right after she died I thought about her constantly."

Amy was silent for a long time. When she turned to Silas, there were tears in her eyes—the first he'd seen. "It's not fair," she whispered. "It's not fair that she's gone and now you're leaving, too."

"Oh, sweetheart," was all he could say as he folded her within his arms. Amy sobbed then. The arms holding her close and the loving endearment were too much. The tears came in a torrent.

Silas continued to hold her and speak quietly to her, stroking her hair and calling her sweetheart. He told her God understood her pain and that He was there for her.

Amy could not remember anything after that. The next day Silas had told her she had cried herself to sleep in his arms. Silas had carried her all the way back to the house and delivered her into the arms of her anxious father who had been watching them from the house.

What Amy did not know, since her father put her to bed and she slept through the night, was that Silas had retired to his room to let his own tears fall. Tears for the 13-year-old boy he had been while watching his mother's body being lowered into the ground. Tears for the 14-year-old girl who had had no siblings with which to share her grief. This young girl who was lonely and scared, who was having to say good-bye to him now that their friendship had become so special.

Amy came out of her reverie when she heard the team and wagon in the yard. For a moment she stood at the kitchen window and wondered what had brought on her memory. She loved it when Silas called her sweetheart. He was the only person who did, and it gave her a special feeling inside. Maybe that was what she wanted—that special feeling. Silas had been so distant for the last few days. Amy told herself he must be homesick. But even as she thought it, she knew it wasn't true. As Amy watched out the window, she thought she saw some white paper in Silas' shirt pocket. She hoped he had gotten a letter from home. That was sure to cheer him up.

Silas spotted Amy at the window, but he kept his face turned away. He had received letters from home, but he hadn't even looked at them. He had also seen Bev Randall in town, and she had given Silas a verbal message for Amy. It was not a happy message and, along with trying to keep his feelings for her hidden, he had the starting of a headache. It looked to be a long evening.

Silas was sure he should wait until tomorrow to deliver his message to Amy, but when Amy said her dad wanted a tray in his room, Silas knew the time was now.

He knew he was acting oddly from the looks Amy kept sending him. She had been eyeing him curiously for the last few days. He was not succeeding in his act, wanting her to believe nothing between them had changed.

The signs of love—watchfulness, the need to be close, wanting to touch—were new to Silas and, because he had to hide them, painful.

Silas had worked at not reaching for her hand or touching her hair more than once in the last few days. The times when Amy had casually touched his arm as she spoke had been torture. Silas wanted to take her small hand in his own and hold it for hours.

Last night Amy had teased him and flicked water in his direction while they were doing the dishes. When she had turned to him, her face wreathed in smiles and laughter, Silas had gripped the dishcloth tightly to keep from grabbing and kissing her.

"Silas, did you hear from home?" The silence between them continued to lengthen as they ate, and Amy could no longer stand it.

"Now, Silas," he said to himself as he faced Amy across the table. "I did get letters from home, but I haven't read them yet." Amy's brow rose in questioning surprise, but she stayed silent.

"I saw your aunt while in town. She sent you a message." Silas' somber tone frightened Amy. "There will be no summer wedding for Thomas Blane and Debra Wheeler because they were married quietly on Monday. She said to tell you that it's not town gossip. She spoke directly to Thomas." Silas paused and his voice dropped low. "Thomas told your aunt that Debra is pregnant; the baby is due in the fall. Mr. Wheeler insisted they move the wedding up and Mrs. Wheeler insisted they live with them until the baby is born.

"Your aunt said she wanted to tell you herself, but felt a message from me was better than waiting and having you possibly hear the news through the gossip lines."

Silas watched as dismay and sadness showed in Amy's eyes. Silas knew that any emotional pain he had previously felt was minimal compared to the pain he felt in knowing the woman he loved was in love with another man.

"I'm sorry, Amy." Silas' voice was husky with raw emotion.

Amy looked at the big, gentle man across from her and knew she had to clarify things for him. He was hurting for her, and she knew that in a few words she could lessen the pain.

"Si, I'm not in love with Thomas. In fact, I've begun to wonder if I ever was. I'm sorry for both Thomas and Debra. In fact, a part of me can understand how easily it could happen. But as painful as Thomas' rejection was, I'm glad we're not married. It obviously would have been a mistake."

Silas felt as though the weight of the earth had been lifted from his shoulders. But his feeling of euphoria didn't last.

"You see, Si, I feel that my dad needs me here. This is my home. My decision not to marry has nothing to do with Thomas breaking off with me. I feel this is God's way of showing me this is where I belong—here, taking care of my father. And even if I had doubts about my feelings, Dad's accident confirmed them. He needs me here."

"Amy does your dad know you feel this way? Somehow I think he would want you to have a home of your own." Silas made no attempt to hide the distress her words caused him.

But Amy didn't take his words personally. "Oh Silas, I know you mean well, but this *is* my home. You're going to think it's silly, but whenever I'm away even for a trip into town, as soon as I spot our farm my heart begins to sing. I know this is where I belong."

"Well Amy, your aunt will be glad you were not overly upset." The statement sounded inane even to his own ears, but he couldn't possibly tell her what he was really thinking.

Amy noticed Silas' surprise upon hearing her beliefs, but she knew she was right. In fact, so sure was she that her mind had already moved back to Thomas and Debra. She didn't even notice when Silas refused dessert and quickly excused himself to check on the cows.

20

Dear Silas,

Baxter is not the same without you. I feel as though you have been gone for months. Josh continually crawls down the hallway to your room and bangs on the closed door.

Luke said the extra work from your absence is not nearly as hard as your missed companionship. Enclosed is a letter from Frank Chambers. He wrote while here to deliver the horses and asked me to send it with mine. Frank took the entire first evening of his visit to try and talk Luke into convincing you to go to work for him in Chicago. Luke heard him out, but told Frank in no uncertain terms that the decision was yours and he would not interfere.

We, of course, want God's will in this, but the thought of you living elsewhere makes me unhappy. We're praying you will know what to do, for this is the only way you'll be at peace.

Please write us. God bless you.

> Love,
>
> Luke, Christine, and Joshua

— ❖ —

Dear Si,

I saddled my horse today and rode down by the creek. I ended up in the spot where we had that huge mud fight as kids. As I recall, Dad warmed our backsides for that one. Sitting in that spot, I missed you so much I cried.

The boys are ready to be out of school for the summer. It shows in their restlessness. Last week Cal locked Charlie in an old trunk in the barn. Their father found them, and I noticed they both sat down carefully at the supper table that night. I guess things never change; each generation gets their share of spankings.

Mac said to tell you Sunday dinner at Gram's is not going to be the same until you come home.

If you don't hear from Sue, it's because she isn't feeling very well these days. She hasn't said, but I suspect she's pregnant.

Please tell the Nolans that we're praying for all of you and that they can't keep you forever.

Love,

Julia and family

— ✤ —

It was the afternoon of the following day before Silas sat down to read his letters. Silas prayed immediately for Sue and the new life possibly growing within her. She and Mark were so happy together that Silas was sure this would only add to their joy.

"Oh God," Silas prayed in his heart, "another niece or nephew. When God? When will I have children of my own? Surely this desire to be a husband and father is from You." Silas sat in painful confusion and tried very hard to thank God for the things he had and not the things missing in his life.

"Be still and know that I am God." The words came gently to Silas. He wasn't even sure of the reference. Maybe somewhere in the Psalms. For the first time, the words became real for him. God was in control. Be still, for He would have His perfect way.

Silas stopped praying. He lay back on his bed and looked toward heaven. Even as he saw the beamed ceiling above him, his heart grew calm and peaceful.

God was in control of Grant, Amy, and him. If Amy was meant to live with her father for the rest of her years, then she and Silas would be miserable as husband and wife. If

Amy was to be his wife, then God would change her heart and Silas would have to learn patience.

"Be still and know that I am God."

"Please God," Silas prayed, "keep those words before my eyes."

Silas lay still for long minutes before he reached for the letter from Frank. He had just started it when Amy called to him. She sounded anxious, and Silas rushed down the stairs.

"Oh Silas, will you help me? Dad has caught a spring cold. He said he would feel better if we put some pillows behind his back." Grant did indeed sound congested, and Silas was glad to do anything to make him more comfortable.

Silas was still in the room when Amy left and returned with a large bottle and spoon. Grant ignored the spoon and took two healthy swigs. Returning the bottle to Amy's hand, Grant said, "This will put me right. Thanks, honey."

Amy followed Silas from the room, taking the bottle with her. Once in the kitchen, Silas noticed she looked a bit pale. He wondered if maybe she was coming down with a cold, too.

"Are you okay?"

"I think so. I'm just a little tired." As Amy spoke, she reached for and began to peel potatoes. Silas was instantly by her side. "Amy, let me get supper so you can rest."

"No Si, you still have the milking to do and it's not fair that you get your own supper." Silas didn't argue with her but decided to get the chores and milking done quickly. He could tell Amy needed help whether she would admit it or not. He checked Grant as he went out and found him soundly sleeping.

Two hours later Silas was just finishing outside. On this of all the nights, when he was in a hurry, everything seemed to go wrong. He'd been kicked twice by an uncooperative cow, and he was not paying attention as he lit a lantern and nearly set the barn ablaze. Those were just a few of the things that delayed his finishing. He moved toward the kitchen, worry for Amy hurrying his steps.

Amy was at the stove when he came in. Strangely, she did not have a greeting for him. Silas washed up in record time and went to her side near the stove. She was looking at a large pot and did not acknowledge his presence.

"Amy, how are you doing?" She did not reply or look at him. "Amy?"

"I can't find my spoon."

Silas picked up a large spoon that was sitting very near her hand. Amy's head came up and, after she focused in on the spoon, her face broke into a huge smile.

Silas saw that her face was flushed and her eyes too bright. "Amy, I think you're sick. Let me do this." The smile turned instantly into a fierce scowl and Amy waved the spoon about as she spoke. "I can do it, Silas. It's my kitchen."

Silas watched as she thrust the spoon into the pot, nearly submerging her hand, and began to stir vigorously.

Silas stood in confusion. Amy was not acting at all like herself, and her speech was slightly slurred. His gaze swung away from her and his eyes caught something on the kitchen table. The large bottle of medicine was sitting open with a wet spoon beside it.

Silas walked toward the bottle with a sinking heart. His head jerked back in repulsion after waving the bottle beneath his nose. Silas was no judge of liquor, but if smell was any indication, the stuff was 90 proof.

Amy was drunk.

Silas quickly set the bottle down and returned to the woman at the stove. Her stirring had slowed down to a methodical movement that seemed to be hypnotizing her. He wondered how much she had taken.

Silas headed for Grant's room. That girl needed to be in bed, and Silas needed some help if nothing more than advice. But Grant was sound asleep, out cold. Silas headed back to the kitchen in consternation.

He arrived to see Amy lift the pot and nearly scald herself. She righted the pot just in time, but Silas' mind was made up. He gave her no time to protest as he took the spoon and pot from her and began to guide her out of the kitchen. But his touch was too light on her arm and she easily pulled away from him, saying as she did that she must finish supper. At least, that's what it sounded like.

Silas tried to reason with her: "Amy, you're sick and should be in bed." But Amy chose to ignore him and tried to get back to the stove.

Silas' next move was to get behind Amy. With his chest to her back and walking slowly, he got her as far as the living room before she turned around and Silas found himself hugging her. At any other time hugging Amy would have delighted him, but his skill with inebriated women was nonexistent and he just wanted to see her safely to her room.

Amy let out a little squeal when Silas gave in and swung her up into his arms. Her head swam and she threw her arms around his neck and closed her eyes.

She did not open them until Silas sat her down on the chest at the end of her bed. Silas hunkered down in front of her and Amy tried hard to concentrate on what he was saying. Everything felt so warm and fuzzy.

"Amy, you need to get ready for bed. I'll get your gown if you tell me where it is." Silas hated even this small intimacy, but he had no choice.

Amy continued to look at him with a small smile on her face, so Silas tried again. "Amy, sweetheart, please try...."

"I love it when you call me sweetheart." Amy's smile grew to just short of a leer.

"Oh boy," Silas thought, "I've got to get out of here or I'm going to kiss her, drunk or not."

Silas' hands flew to Amy's shoes, removing them quickly. A fast search of the room produced Amy's robe and nightgown from the hook on the back of the door. When he set the garments beside her, she informed him that some beast was wrapped around her waist. Silas unknotted the apron strings she had been demolishing and pulled her quickly to her feet.

He thrust the clothing into her arms and commanded, "Put these on, Amy. Now!" With that he exited the room, nearly slamming the door in his haste.

Silas leaned back against the closed door and prayed. He heard bumping sounds from in the room, and then Amy broke into song.

Silas rolled his eyes toward the ceiling and headed for Grant's room. He was still very deep in sleep.

All was quiet in Amy's room as Silas returned to stand outside the door. He waited a moment in indecision and then quietly opened the door.

Amy lay across the bed in her nightgown and robe humming to herself. She raised her head, and Silas could see she was very sleepy.

With utmost care, Silas pulled the covers back and lifted her into his arms. He tucked her within the blankets, robe and all. She was asleep before Silas could straighten. He stood looking at her a moment, wishing he could tell her what was in his heart, before quietly leaving the room.

21

The small copse of trees had seemed like a good hiding place the night before when running from an outraged farmer with a shotgun. But as dawn began to light the sky, the joints and muscles of both men were doubting the wisdom of their decision.

"You think it's safe?"

"Yea, I just hope nobody found the horses."

"If we're gonna get shot at, I'm gonna ask for more money."

"You just let me do the talkin', little brother. You go shooting your mouth off, and we'll be out of work fast."

"Okay, okay, I just don't like sleeping out of my bed. Makes me sore for days."

"Stop whining. We got the money and that means we get paid. Come on, let's get back to town."

— ✢ —

Silas moved slowly in an attempt to relieve the ache in his back, brought on by a night on the living room sofa. The piece of furniture was neither long enough nor wide enough to support his frame, and he had found little rest upon it.

The night before Silas had made sure that both bedroom doors were open. Amy had slept through the night, but Grant had stirred twice. Silas had seen to his comfort both times and once had given him more medicine.

Grant had shown no pity on Silas when he described Amy's bout with the medicine. He laughed and told Silas that a man who had been allowed to stay the night in the barn a few years ago had given it to him. The man swore it would knock a cold or flu right out of your system.

Grant had not had any suspicions about the contents until his next cold. But it had worked so fast that he didn't care what was in it.

Amy, to his knowledge, had never used it. But then, she rarely got sick. He had asked Silas to check on her then for his peace of mind. Silas had found her warm, but not alarmingly so. Knowing Amy was fine, Grant had gone back to sleep with the help of more medicine. Silas had returned to his temporary bed in the living room and asked God to heal both father and daughter quickly.

Now it was time to do the milking and, with a quick check on both his sleeping patients, Silas headed outside.

— ✛ —

Amy stretched and squirmed under the heaviness of the bed covers. Something felt strange to her, but she was too sleepy to figure it out. Well, at least her head was clear. Last night as she was fixing supper she knew she had caught a cold along with her dad. She could not believe how fast her head had stuffed up.

On impulse, she had taken some of his medicine and, being unsure of the proper dosage, had drunk several tablespoons. Amy's mind stopped in confusion then. The rest of the evening seemed rather vague.

No worry, really, she thought. It had obviously done the trick with as good as she felt. With a sweep of her arm, she threw back the quilts and swung her feet to the floor.

She stared down at her feet in surprise when she noticed she still had one stocking on. Catching sight of herself in the big oval mirror over her dresser, Amy saw that the extra weight in her bed had been her robe and that her hair was still pinned up.

A sudden vision of Silas carrying her through the door and then of him untying her apron at the foot of the bed made Amy's eyes go wide. She began to notice small things.

The curtains were not pulled closed and her clothes were thrown all over the room. And her Bible—it was closed. She always opened her Bible to the place where she was reading so she could reach right for it, first thing in the morning.

She reached for it now, and it somehow gave her comfort. "Oh God," she prayed, "You know what I'm thinking, but it just can't be true. Silas would never do that."

Amy was by nature a levelheaded girl. She now used some of her logic to calm herself. She would go about her normal routine and simply ask Silas when she saw him.

Amy dressed, made her bed, and read her Bible. After she closed her father's door to give him quiet, breakfast was the next step in her routine.

But all Amy's coolheaded thinking flew out the window when Silas came in from milking. Before even washing up, he came toward her with a wide smile and asked how she felt.

To Amy's embarrassment, she blushed a fiery red and blurted out, "Silas, how did I get to bed last night?"

Horror overcame her as Silas' own cheeks turned pink and he stared down at the toes of his boots. "Oh no," Amy's mind protested.

When Silas looked up, he knew immediately what she was thinking. "No, Amy, no." Silas was equally horrified. "I just helped you with your shoes and apron. You got yourself ready for bed. You were falling asleep on top of the quilts and I tucked you in. I swear that was all."

Amy looked relieved but still embarrassed. "I guess Dad's medicine is a bit strong."

For the first time Silas saw humor in the situation, and his grin clearly showed his amusement. "You, Miss Nolan, were quite drunk last night."

Amy eyed him warily and asked, "What did I say?"

"Ah, now that would be telling."

"Silas Cameron," Amy scolded, "how dare you tease me about something so embarrassing."

Silas laughed then and assured her she had been a perfect lady. Amy did not look completely convinced, but she couldn't have been too upset for she served him an enormous breakfast and they talked like old friends during the meal.

22

The next weeks were spent in long hours of planting. As long as there was light in the sky, Silas was in the fields. Amy was back to doing most of the milking.

Silas worked out a deal with the man from the cheese factory who always picked up the Nolan's milk. The man would haul the cans—not Amy. Amy protested, but Silas was adamant.

Silas had been furious to discover the man had let her do all the hauling for the two weeks prior to Silas' arrival. They argued about it one day after the man left.

"I can't believe he let you haul those cans. Can he really be that lazy?"

"Yes, I'm afraid he can."

"Did your dad know about this?"

"Honestly, Silas, Dad had enough on his mind. I am a big girl, you know, and I can take care of myself."

This was the real rub, and Silas knew it. He wanted it to be his place to take care of her. The subject was dropped, but it continued to bother Silas.

— ❖ —

Silas had finally read his letter from Frank Chambers. As expected, he had not accepted the refusal Silas sent before he came to Neillsville.

With the farm work and emotional changes going on in Silas' life he had given very little thought to Frank's offer, even though Christine had warned him of the man's persistency. He needed to continue in prayer regarding that offer. Frank had said to take his time and think it over. With all the unsettled things in Silas' life right now, he needed to do just that.

Silas' relationship with Amy was good, if not as comfortable as it once was. Silas smiled wryly to himself at the different way a man thinks of his little sister and the way he thinks of the woman he wants for his wife.

Little things he had never noticed about Amy before were becoming very dear to him: the way she chewed her lower lip whenever she was anxious about something; the way her voice took on a childlike quality as she prayed, so trusting and sweet; her concentration and sparkling eyes whenever she played the piano. These and so much more made up the whole of Amy.

Amy. Amy Cameron. Silas had tried the name out loud one day in the barn when there was no one to hear but the cows. He loved the way it sounded, but not knowing if it would ever come to pass was disheartening. He tried not to dwell on it.

He petitioned God constantly to give him strength and wisdom in this situation where he felt so helpless. Silas was unable to see it right now, but this time in his life was bringing him closer and closer to God.

There were even moments when he felt God had forgotten him, but they were brief. For even amid the pain of wishing for a life with Amy and not knowing if he would ever have it, was a sweet, peaceful knowledge that God had not deserted him and that His will for Silas was perfect and complete.

23

Grant was getting stronger every day. Each evening he and Silas talked about the planting and Grant was able to give much advice and encouragement from his many years in the fields. He fretted some, too, at not being able to man the plow himself.

The difference in the men's ages came home hard to Grant when Silas reported each night how much he was able to do in a day. Even with Grant's best team, those days were behind him.

But truthfully, he was not really very envious. He just asked God to let him walk again. This he prayed for with his whole heart.

Doctor Schaefer had been pleased with how well Grant had come out of his cold, but was worried nevertheless. He told Grant he wanted to see him up in a chair, increasing the time each day as he felt stronger. Doc informed them that he had lost more patients from a bedridden state because of their chest filling up, than by deaths resulting directly from accidents such as Grant's.

It was during one of these times with Silas in the field and Grant sitting in the living room that father and daughter were able to talk.

Amy had just walked some food and water out to Silas—the last he would get until he came in for supper. When she returned, Grant asked how things were going. Knowing how close it was to milking, he was surprised when Amy settled into a seat.

"It's going well, I think. Silas can sure cover a lot of ground in a day."

"Yes, he's a lot faster than your old dad."

"I never think of you as old, Dad," Amy said softly and then fell quiet. Grant waited and hoped. Amy would never know how long he had prayed for this time.

"There is something I have wanted to talk to you about Dad, but I'm afraid you'll be upset."

"A parent has to be careful not to make any promises with a statement like that, but I will hear you out."

Amy studied the man across from her. His sandy-brown hair was liberally streaked with gray. There were laugh lines at the corners of his eyes, and his skin was a permanent shade of red from years in the sun.

He was a wonderful father, and Amy knew he loved her dearly. Yes, he would hear her out; he'd always been fair.

Without introduction Amy began. "Uncle Evan asked me to come into town and live with them." Amy paused, but Grant said nothing. Other than a slight lift of his eyebrows, his expression didn't alter.

"I knew when he asked me that I didn't want to, but I was so surprised I didn't say a word. And then the last time I was with him, he said something that really bothered me. He said if my father really loved me he'd let me go. I've known for a long time that there was no friendship between you two, but I can't stand the thought of having Uncle Evan believe the reason I'm saying no is because you won't let me go."

"Should you say no?" The question was spoken so calmly that Amy could only stare at her father.

"You mean you want me to go?"

"I want you to be wherever God leads you. As much as I'd miss you, I know Evan and Bev would take good care of you."

"But Dad, what about you? Who would take care of you?"

"Amy, honey, you must not build your life around me. What did you think would happen to me when you and Thomas moved into your own home—that I would wither up and die?"

"Well no, but Dad I just figured that the breakup with Thomas was God's way of saying, 'Stay here and take care of your father.'"

"Amy, do you really think me that selfish? I've been where you are—young and ready for love, and I found that love. Your mother and I loved one another deeply and when God gave us you, there wasn't anything more in the world we would have asked for.

"I want you to experience the things that I have—marriage and family. I can't imagine a man wanting a more wonderful wife than you would be. And when it comes to babies, well I've seen your face light up when you hold them at church.

"You know I'll respect your decision about living in town or not, and there are no words to describe how much I would miss you if you go. But Amy, do not, *do not* base your decisions on a need to stay here and take care of me."

"But it's not just that. This is a good life here. I love it on this farm."

"You're right—it is a good life, we've been blessed many times over. But God may have a completely different plan for you, Amy, and I'll not hold you back."

There was silence in the room for a long time. Grant's compassion for his only child was great and, even though his words had shocked her, they needed to be said.

Amy stood. "I best get to the barn." Grant nodded. Amy hesitated and then walked to his chair. They hugged long and hard. "This is the only home I've ever known."

"I know, honey, and I'm not pushing you out, but please don't close your eyes to what God might have for you beyond these acres."

Amy stepped back and held her father's hand. She squeezed gently and said, "Thanks, Dad." On these words she moved for the door.

24

The following day was Saturday, and Silas came in from the fields a bit early. Amy surprised both men at the supper table when she asked if Silas would take her to town after the meal. Silas assured her he would be glad to oblige. Amy then looked to Grant.

"You're sure, Amy?"

"I'm sure. I should have told Uncle Evan the first day he asked me."

Amy did a quick cleanup on the kitchen and they were able to leave while there was still light in the sky.

Neillsville on Saturday night was a busy place. In front of each saloon was a crowd, and the noise spoke of boisterous activity within. Amy was glad for Silas' presence. A man would have to be crazy to challenge someone of Silas' proportions—crazy or drunk.

Amy wondered a little at her decision to come into town at night, but she knew it was time to resolve this with Uncle Evan. She had prayed about little else since her talk with her dad and knew without a doubt the answer to her uncle must be no. If Amy was honest with herself, she did not really believe she would ever move away from the farm. The only reason she could think of would be to marry, and there were simply no men in the area in whom she was the least bit interested. She knew her father meant well, but for now just knowing she would be able to settle things was peace enough.

The entire downstairs of the Randall mansion was lit. For a moment Amy thought her relations might be entertaining, but the carriage house was closed and there did not seem to be any extra vehicles about.

For the second time in Silas' visit, he and Amy stood in silence at the Randalls' front door. Silas did not need to ask how Amy was feeling. Her attempt at gnawing her lower lip off was answer enough.

Bev Randall was surprised but also very pleased to see Amy. She greeted Silas warmly and, after seating them in her elegant living room, rang for refreshments.

After the servant left them, Amy wasted no time in stating her purpose. "Aunt Bev, is Uncle Evan here?"

"No dear, he went out for awhile. He didn't say where he was going, so I really have no idea when he planned to return."

Amy looked as distressed as she felt. "Is there something I can do, Amy?"

"Well, I'm not sure. I think I should tell Uncle Evan first but I..." Amy's voice trailed away in uncertainty.

"Is it about your coming to live here?"

Amy nodded.

"Evan told me that he'd asked you."

"You mean he didn't discuss it with you before he talked with me?"

"Amy dear, your uncle rarely sees fit to discuss anything with me." Bev smiled, but Amy thought she caught a trace of bitterness in her aunt's words.

"I'm sorry he didn't discuss it with you first. He should have," Amy stated firmly and went on before Bev could interrupt. "I've come tonight to tell him no. I know the offer was made in love, but I want to stay on the farm. I've never had a strong desire to live in town. I know Uncle Evan will think my dad is holding me back, but that's not true. The farm is where I want to be and would be even if Dad had not been hurt."

A servant entered the room then and served small sandwiches and cookies for three. Amy's plate of food sat untouched, and she was quiet a moment as she sipped her coffee.

"Aunt Bev, I really wanted to give my answer to Uncle Evan. Please don't be hurt, but I need to be able to express how I feel to him in person."

"I'll not even tell him you were here," she stated in kind assurance. "You can tell him the next time you see him."

"You're not hurt?"

"No, I'm glad for the special relationship you have with Evan. You make your uncle very happy." Amy knew the words were sincere, and she felt some relief from her heavy task.

They stayed awhile longer with Silas joining into the conversation. Evan did not arrive before they left, and Amy resigned herself to the fact that she would have to deliver her answer to Evan Randall another time.

25

Amy played the piano and sang a solo the following morning in church. Feeling his chest expand in pride, Silas watched her. Her gifts of singing and playing were beautiful as she used them to give glory to God.

Silas immersed himself into the sermon in 2 John that morning. Pastor Johnson dwelt especially on the point of walking in the truth to show our love to God. Near the end of the message he spoke to the unbeliever.

"Allow me to repeat some of what I've said and speak to those of you who may not truly know of the love I've been speaking on.

"The way we show our love to God is to walk in the truth. This means obedience to the Bible and the commandments written within. The Scripture says, 'We love him because he first loved us.' What is this first love? Salvation. The greatest example of love was God sending His Son, Jesus Christ, to die for us. He took our sins; He is our salvation. Until you understand this act of love, your sin divides you from God. Christ's death on the cross covers that divide, bridges that space.

"I quote this verse to you often, but if you haven't ever reached out to God, you need to hear it again. John 3:16: 'For God so loved the world, that he gave his only begotten Son, that whosoever believeth in him should not perish, but have everlasting life.'"

Amy played the piano for the altar call at the end of the service, and a little girl came forward with her mother. They both looked a little frightened, and Silas' heart went out to them even as he hoped they would come to a saving knowledge of Christ that morning.

When the service ended, it seemed most of the congregation was of a mind to stand and visit. One of the women from town said there had been another robbery the night before.

Unable to stop the shudder running through her, Amy thought of her and Silas out after dark. As frightened as she was by the talk, she couldn't stop herself from listening.

"They all seem to be related to the bank. When someone makes a withdrawal, his money is taken."

"How many robberies have there been?"

"I think about 20."

"Twenty? I heard it was more like 30."

"Well, I think someone at the bank is involved. I want to withdraw my money, but I'm afraid we'll get robbed, too."

"We should all go in together. They can't rob all of us."

"Yes, that's it. We've all got to band togeth..."

A large hand gently took Amy's arm and led her from the circle. No one within the group seemed to notice her presence, nor did they see her leaving.

"Silas did you hear—"

"Shhh, sweetheart. Let's get to the wagon." Amy allowed herself to be led to the wagon and be lifted to the seat as though she were a child.

She couldn't believe they were talking about the bank with such anger. Uncle Evan did not have many friends, but he would never... but where had he been last night? Aunt Bev had not even known.

Shame engulfed Amy over what she was thinking. How dare she or any of the women at the church judge Evan Randall.

Amy started when the wagon stopped. They were not home yet, and Amy looked to Silas questioningly.

"Talk to me, Amy. I only heard part of what the women were saying."

When she had finished, Silas exclaimed "Thirty robberies? Amy don't you see that in their panic the facts are being blown completely out of proportion? Your uncle is not the most social of men, but you're right—no one has grounds to call him a thief."

"What if everyone does want their money?"

"I don't know. If there was another robbery last night, I have a feeling this whole affair is going to come to a boil in the next few days."

Silas' prediction was partially right. Things did come to a head, but it didn't take a few days.

Evan Randall's small, gleaming black buggy, pulled by an equally black horse, drove into the Nolan farmyard the very next night.

Evan had not been to the farm since Maureen had died, over four years ago. Knowing this, Amy did not move to the front door in joy but with an awful feeling of dread growing in the pit of her stomach.

"Good evening, Amy. I'm sorry to burst in on you like this, but I need to speak with your father." There was none of the softness that he usually had for Amy. His voice was brisk, and his words to the point.

"Of course, Uncle Evan. Please come in."

Grant was sitting in the living room, and it was obvious to the younger people that their presence was not needed.

Amy and Silas headed outside to the porch to wait and be out of the way. They were both surprised at how quickly Evan reappeared and was on his way to the buggy.

Amy stood in silent confusion. Evan was seated before he looked up and seemed to realize she was standing there. He maneuvered his rig close to the porch and, ignoring Silas, spoke directly to his niece.

"You must understand, Amy, that nothing between us has changed. I care for you deeply, as I always have." His tone was very businesslike. "I'm sure you'll see that I had little choice." He paused here, and Amy could see genuine regret in his eyes. "It grieves me to withdraw my offer of you living with us, but things have become very complicated in the last few hours and I feel right now it would be best if we postpone the offer indefinitely. Good night, Amy. Please don't hesitate to visit. You know you'll always be welcome in my home."

Without giving her a chance to reply, he turned the buggy sharply and rode away. Silas and Amy stared after him and then at each other.

They found Grant in the chair they'd left him in, but he was slumped low and seemed to have aged years in the few minutes they were outside.

He looked at Amy as he spoke. "There's been a run on the bank and Evan has called in our loan. I've got a week to come up with the money."

26

Forty-eight hours after Grant had uttered those devastating words, Amy was on the verge of panic. Trying not to pace, she waited for Silas to come from her father's bedroom, but she couldn't sit still.

The night Evan visited, Grant had briefly told them what he'd come to say. Evidently, in a panic, about half of the bank patrons had come in on Monday morning demanding their money. A few were large depositors. If not for those, the bank would have stood its own. As it was, Grant felt Evan had panicked a little himself by calling Grant's loan and two others.

After some discussion Monday night, the subject had been dropped. Now Amy waited for Silas who had gone into Grant's room after supper to see if something could be worked out.

When he appeared in the kitchen, Amy was seated. She frantically wrung her hands and asked, "Is Dad okay?"

Silas was surprised at her state of agitation. He had not realized how upset she was. "Oh Silas, what are we to do? What was Uncle Evan thinking? We don't have money put aside to pay off that loan. Does he think we're hiding it in our mattresses?"

"Amy, try to calm down. I need to tell you something."

"Calm? You want me to be calm? The only home I've ever known is about to be taken from me and you ask me to be calm?"

"But Amy, if you would just listen, your dad and I have talked and I'd like to tell you if you would just simmer down."

"Silas, you never answered my question. Is Dad okay? Oh, never mind. I'll check on him myself."

Silas caught her at the door. "Amy, come back to the table and let me talk to you. I didn't realize you were so upset."

"You didn't realize I was upset?" she nearly shouted at him as he led her back into the room. "Well, what did you think I'd be with all that's happen..."

Amy's words were abruptly cut off as Silas snatched her into his arms and covered her mouth firmly with his own.

The kiss was not short, and Silas felt Amy go limp in his arms as his lips tenderly held hers. Amy gasped when Silas broke the kiss, and her eyes rivaled the moon for size.

While still holding her, Silas' soft, deep voice broke into the now-quiet kitchen. "If you will just sit down and stay quiet for a moment, I'll tell you about my conversation with your dad."

On Amy's nod, Silas released her and sat at the table. Silas took a chair near hers. "Your dad and I have talked, and I offered him what I have in my savings. It's not the full amount of the loan, but close enough that I think Evan will take it. We've still got a few days, so your dad wants to think and pray on it some."

Amy was moved nearly to tears and still in shock over what had just transpired, but she managed to say, "Thank you, Silas," in a small voice.

They sat in silence then. Silas studied his hands, his face expressionless. He looked up to find Amy concentrating on his mouth, and he spoke without thinking. "Did Thomas ever kiss you?"

Amy jerked as though struck and turned red. "Yes, t-twice after w-we w-were engaged." Amy realized she was stuttering and stopped in painful embarrassment. But Silas still looked at her, and she wished she knew what he was thinking.

A terrible thought coming to her, Amy asked in a harsh whisper, "Silas, are you disgusted with me? Do you think I'm cheap for kissing Thomas?"

Pain slashed across Silas' features at her words, and his voice was rough with emotion. "Never, Amy, would I think you cheap. It's only natural that you kiss the man you expect to marry."

Amy was so relieved that she nearly wept. She could not have stood it if Silas was repulsed by her.

The silence between them lengthened and grew uncomfortable. Finally Amy asked, "Would you like some coffee or anything?"

"No thanks. I think I'll go check the herd and then turn in." He spoke the words softly and for the first time did not attempt to hide what was in his heart.

Amy's own heart thumped furiously at what she read in his eyes. For just an instant their eyes held, and then Silas pushed away from the table and strode toward the door.

— ✠ —

Grant listened in alarm as Amy's raised voice came from the other room. Silas said something in return, but Grant couldn't make out the words.

Grant froze as Amy's voice nearly raised to a shout before all went completely quiet. He continued to listen, and after a while heard the front door open and close.

Grant relaxed back against the pillows, a smile on his face. If he were a betting man, he'd place money on the fact that Amy had just been kissed.

He wondered how rough the road ahead would be. It was only a matter of time until Amy stopped mothering him and saw that the man she needed most was sitting beneath her nose. And Silas was probably sure he had just been sent by God to work in the fields, figuring Amy would never return his love.

Well, Grant knew he could not interfere. God would lead the way. "But please, Lord," he prayed, "let me be on my feet to walk her down the aisle."

— ✠ —

You're a fool, Silas Cameron. The biggest fool to ever live. Silas had been saying this and worse for the past two hours.

He had every line and splinter on the ceiling memorized as he lay in bed.

He should not have been trying to think at all for he was exhausted physically as well as emotionally. Weeks of working in the fields were taking their toll. Silas was beginning to think the life of a horse breeder was a life of ease. He was sure Luke would argue that point since he was carrying all the weight and had been for many weeks.

It was time to go home. The planting was done, and as soon as they worked out the money details there would be no reason to stay.

The savings would be missed. Silas had been praying about building his own home this summer, but Grant and Amy needed the money more. And since he didn't have a wife and kids, he had no real need for a home of his own.

No home or family of his own—that was the real reason he had to go. He had all but told Amy of his feelings. There was no way she would be comfortable around him now. At least before they had shared a friendship, but now he was even unsure of that.

Amy had made her feelings quite clear about marriage and her home here. She was more than a little attached to this farm—perhaps too much so, but he wouldn't want to take her away if she didn't want to go.

Silas lay awake for a long time thinking and praying. It was clear to him he had been used of God in the lives of these people, and for this he was thankful. But he was human, with human emotions, and was saddened at knowing his heart belonged to a woman who could not give hers in return.

It was a long time before Silas fell asleep.

Her hand going to her mouth continually, Amy could still feel Silas' kiss. Thomas had kissed her—twice, once passionately. But nothing had ever prepared her for being in the arms of Silas Cameron. Amy felt herself blushing with the remembrance.

Burying her face in the pillow, she could still see his eyes. "He's in love with me." The words were muffled and indistinct. "But he can't love me," she tried to reason with herself. "I'm like a little sister to him. Somewhere along the line, those feelings must have changed.

"And what about my feelings? His kiss made me feel like I was melting. But we're just friends. Can good friends fall in love? I don't know.

"Well it doesn't matter," she reasoned suddenly. "I have to stay here and take care of my dad. If I was in love with Silas, he would want to take me to Baxter and my dad needs me here."

"Do not build your life around me." Unbidden, her father's selfless words came to mind, but Amy pushed them away. He was just saying that! This was her home and he needed her here!

Amy snuggled deep into the covers with a contented sigh. It was going to be hard to have Silas' feelings stronger than her own, but this was where she was supposed to be, she was sure.

Amy fell asleep without remembering to open her Bible. In fact, in all her logic Amy didn't check with God at all.

27

Amy was seeing Doc Schaefer out, so Silas took the opportunity to speak with Grant alone. Silas was beginning to think Grant was a mind reader when he stepped into the bedroom and Grant said, "Shut the door, Silas. I want to talk with you."

When Silas was seated in the rocking chair near the bed, Grant seemed at a loss for words. He cleared his throat twice, and still he hesitated. Silas knew he was about to be thanked, and so he stepped in, hoping to put it off.

"I'd like to come back, Grant."

"Come back?"

"Yes. I have every confidence that you'll be back on your feet, but I'd still like to come back and give you a hand."

"You don't have to do that, Silas." Grant was very pleased with the offer, but this young man had already done so much.

"Actually, Grant, I'd be returning for selfish reasons. This is the first planting I've done on my own, and I'd like to see the fruits of my labors."

The older man's hand came out and they shook. "Thanks, Silas. I'll count on you. You come when you can."

"I'll wait until my brother-in-law Mac starts his harvesting, and then I'll write that I'm coming." Silas stood to go. "Oh, ah, one more thing, Grant. Please don't say anything to Amy about my coming back. I'd like to do that myself."

"Sure, Silas. I understand." The men nodded to one another in understanding, and Silas exited the room.

— ✤ —

Silas sat despondently at the supper table and watched Amy look at everything but him. Even if he put a question to her directly, she answered his chin, never once looking him in the eye.

119

Grant didn't miss the byplay between Silas and his daughter, and he struggled to hold his tongue. He knew that whatever was between them they would have to work out. Nevertheless he would not stand for Amy being rude to Silas or making him feel unwelcome in their home.

When Silas refused both a second helping of supper and dessert and excused himself from the table, Grant determined to talk with Amy. But once they were alone, Amy gave up all pretense of eating and sat looking at the door Silas had just walked through. Just the pain written on his daughter's face was enough to stay any comment Grant had been ready to make.

Amy was miserable. She knew Silas was hurting and the relationship they'd known was changed, possibly forever. Also, Silas was leaving tomorrow, and guilt lay heavy on Amy's heart for the relief she felt. What was the matter with her? How could she be so cruel? If only Silas' feelings hadn't changed and they could have stayed just friends.

Amy would probably have sat at the table toying with her food all evening, but Silas appeared in the doorway.

"I'm not positive, but I believe Bev Randall is coming this way." Amy rushed to the window, and Grant craned his neck to try and see.

Amy turned back to the room. "It *is* Aunt Bev." She paused and then added, "I'm not sure I want to know why she's here."

"Well," Grant spoke briskly to cover his own feeling of trepidation, "that won't change the fact that she is. If someone will help me into the living room, we'll find out what's going on." Silas moved to assist him. For all Grant's businesslike words, Silas thought he looked worried.

Clearly in a state of high agitation, Bev Randall would not take a seat. She paced back and forth as Grant sat watching her in bewilderment.

"I was just furious when he told me. I stood up to Evan for the first time." Here she stopped in front of Grant and faced him squarely. "I told him to reinstate your loan or I'd be on the next train out of town."

"Oh Bev, you didn't!" Grant was truly horrified. As harsh as Evan's actions had been, nothing was worth Bev and Evan's marriage.

"Yes I did, and I'm not sorry. Evan never tells me anything until the act is complete, or we could have avoided all of this."

Bev had resumed her pacing, but again she stopped and put a trembling hand to her throat. "I never dreamed he would do such a thing. That you should suffer for..."

A short silence hung in the room. "Well," Bev visibly composed herself. Once again the elegant banker's wife was firmly back in place. "You're going to think me a fishwife, screeching and stomping about. Now, Amy, I do believe I could do with a cup of coffee."

"Oh, of course, Aunt Bev." Amy jumped up to do her bidding, still in a state of shock over all that had transpired.

Bev stayed a long time and told them of the situation in town. "The townspeople this week have been out of their heads, storming the bank, sure that Evan was taking their money. There were stories of 40 robberies, if you can imagine. Their panic was so great, yet no one had a single fact. They were shouting at the sheriff for justice and, believe it or not, he came to the bank's rescue. He's a good man, you know.

"Well, he told the bank patrons he had a full-scale investigation going on and that things were under control. He had already collected some valuable evidence, and none of it pointed to anyone at the bank. He was also putting extra men on the job in an attempt to curtail the thefts."

Bev left soon after her report, and Amy cleared away the cups before joining Silas and Grant in the living room. They sat and talked some, but each was emotionally drained and it wasn't long before they were all seeking their beds and thanking God for a miracle in the form of Bev Randall.

28

Silas would have given much to go to the train station alone, but that would have left a horse in town for Amy to pick up and he did not want that.

Arriving at the station, Silas assured Amy she need not stay, but she insisted. Now they stood on the station platform in painful silence, Silas towering over her, each one with so much and yet nothing to say.

The train rumbled in the distance and Silas knew he had to tell Amy of his plans to return. "Amy, I need to tell you something." Amy stiffened, mistaking his intention, and would not raise her eyes to his.

"Amy, please look at me." She did slowly, afraid of what she would see, but to her surprise Silas, the big brother, stared down at her.

"I'm coming back in the fall to help with the harvest. I think your dad will be up and around, but I want to give him a hand."

Amy was obviously surprised. "You're always so thoughtful, Silas. Thank you very much."

The train was coming into the station, and Silas raised his voice slightly to be heard. "Well, thank you for everything. I'll see you in the fall." Giving her a quick hug, he was saddened at how stiff she was in his arms.

He broke the hug, but couldn't bring himself to stop touching her. His hands lightly held her shoulders and he looked down at her tenderly.

"I'm still your friend, Amy." Silas couldn't hold back the words. "And should you ever need me, I'll come."

Amy could only stare at him, and Silas felt her relax beneath his hands. Moving slowly and giving her plenty of time to move away, Silas bent his head and brushed her lips with his own.

When he broke the kiss, he was still so close Amy could feel his breath on her cheek. "Good-bye sweetheart." His voice was a strained, husky whisper.

Amy stood on the platform and watched until the train was out of sight. Relieved that Silas was gone, she was also glad he was returning. When he came back she was sure their old relationship would be restored, and even now she looked forward to the time. He was hurt now, but they would be friends again—of this Amy was determined.

Of course, he might meet a nice girl this summer and get married before he returned. Amy refused to ask herself why this idea was not really very appealing.

29

Baxter, Wisconsin

Grandma Em silently watched Silas across her kitchen table and wondered again what had really gone on in Neillsville. It had taken her a few minutes when he had arrived the night before to get used to him without a beard. After studying him a few moments, she decided she liked it very much.

But more than just Silas' physical appearance had changed. They had talked, sharing all the latest news, but something was not quite right. Amid the family news confirming Sue's pregnancy, Luke's hard work, and how much the nieces and nephews had missed him, Silas was strangely preoccupied.

Silas had shared briefly of his stay in Neillsville and, in so doing, made Gramdma Em even more sure that something was not right. He talked of the Nolans, the crops, the size of the church, the robberies and the bank run, and even someone named Thomas who was now married to Debra.

Grandma Em's mind kept returning to those two, wondering if they were somehow a key as to why Silas seemed upset. Silas evidently thought she knew who they were. But she didn't and wondered what they had to do with Silas' stay at the Nolans. She hoped in time he would talk to her of what he was really feeling or, to be specific, the real reason the sparkle had gone out of his eyes.

"Gram, is there more coffee?"

"Yes, I could use some myself. I'll get it for you." After she poured the coffee she remarked, "I haven't read my Bible yet. Would you like to join me?"

Silas smiled. "You know I would."

She read from Psalm 1:1-3.

Blessed is the man that walketh not in the counsel of the ungodly, nor standeth in the way of sinners, nor sitteth in the seat of the scornful. But his delight is in the law of the Lord; and in his law doth he meditate day and night. And he shall be like a tree planted by the rivers of water, that bringeth forth his fruit in his season; his leaf also shall not wither; and whatsoever he doeth shall prosper.

They prayed together and then shared another cup of coffee.

"How are you planning to get home?" Grandma Em asked.

"Well now, I've been thinking on that. I might just walk."

Grandma Em looked surprised. "Silas, I know very well the hard work involved in getting a crop in. You can't really be needing more exercise."

"No," he laughed, "I just thought it might be nice. It is a pretty day."

Grandma Em wasn't fooled and could no longer keep her silence. "What's her name, Silas?"

"Am I that transparent?"

Grandma Em didn't answer, not having been sure until that moment if she was on the right track.

"Her name is Amy Nolan."

"I take it you found she was no longer 14."

"No, she is definitely not 14. I almost wish she were."

"Does she know how you feel?"

"Yes, I'm afraid I gave myself away just before I left. It was the last thing I wanted. We're such good friends, and now she is no longer even comfortable around me. I don't want her hurt."

"But you're hurting yourself, Silas." Grandma Em's voice was filled with compassion.

"You're right—I do hurt. I hurt in a way I didn't know was possible. I love her, Gram. I want her for my wife, but to her I'm just a big brother and she is sure Grant would never get along without her. Her plan is to live at home the rest of her life."

The two fell again into silence and then Silas said, "I'm going back. I told Grant I would come and help get his crops in. And when I go, I'll try to repair our friendship. I'll try to put things right."

"Maybe being separated for the summer will help."

"Maybe," Silas sounded unconvinced even to himself. He missed Amy already.

"Well, I better start home."

"Yes, you better. Christine will be delighted to see you. She said it's been painfully obvious that Josh's favorite toy is missing."

Smiling, Silas felt his heart lighten some. Even the ache in his heart did not diminish the joy of knowing he was almost home.

30

The walk home worked like a tonic on Silas. He was glad that most of the way was beyond the houses of town because he couldn't wipe the smile from his face. Anyone watching would have thought him dim-witted.

Silas felt not at all fatigued as he neared the ranch. In fact, when the house came into view, he began to run. Just as he hit the porch, the front door opened and Christine ran out. Silas grabbed her in a great hug, and Christine laughed with sheer joy.

"Your beard!" Christine cried. She was staring at him, her mouth wide open. "I can't believe you shaved your beard off! You look wonderful!"

"Well, I'm glad you approve. For a minute there I wondered if you might not."

"It's just that you look so different. My goodness, you're almost as good-looking as Luke."

Silas laughed. "Now that's high praise coming from a woman in love. By the way, where is the man in question?"

"He's right here," a deep voice sounded behind them, "trying to figure out who the strange, beardless man hugging my woman is." Luke came up the steps, and the two brothers embraced.

"You know," Luke commented, "I'd forgotten what you look like under all that fur. You're not half bad-looking."

"Thanks," Silas said dryly, but he was grinning.

"Where's Josh?" Silas asked of Christine.

"He's inside. Come on. Did you walk from the train station?"

"No, I walked from Grandma Em's. I got in last night."

"Josh, look who's here."

Joshua Cameron was sitting on the kitchen floor contentedly chewing on a hard biscuit. Christine scooped him up, washed the crumbs from his face and hands, and landed him in the arms of his Uncle Silas.

Silas held this treasured little boy and said nothing. He actually expected Joshua to reach for Christine, but for the moment Josh just sat looking solemnly up at the man holding him.

Silas returned Josh's solemn appraisal, looking deep into the inherited brilliance of the Cameron blue eyes.

"Hi, Josh." Still no change in expression. But Silas didn't care—it just felt so good to hold him. Josh's little hand reached up and tentatively touched Silas' mustache. Silas held still as the tiny fingers explored his upper lip and the hair above it. Suddenly Josh giggled.

The adults laughed, too, and Silas hugged the little boy fiercely to himself. His heart nearly burst with happiness. These people were his home.

— ✤ —

Dear Frank,

I realize I have taken a long time getting back to you and I appreciate your patience. The job you offered me sounds wonderful, and I am greatly complimented you believe me capable, but I must turn the offer down.

I do not answer you lightly. I have prayed long and hard over this, and for this reason I'm certain I should stay where I am.

I hope we will continue to do business and remain well-acquainted in the years to come. Luke and I both greatly respect your knowledge and wisdom in our trade.

Again, my thanks and hopes you will soon find a man to take on the position.

Sincerely,
Silas Cameron

Silas felt instant peace settle over him upon completion of the letter. Sitting at the desk in his room, he bowed his head.

"Heavenly Father, thank You for giving me wisdom in this job offer. I could not gain perfect peace about it, and so I believe Your answer is no. Thank You, God, for this home and my work here. Please help me to know if I should build this year. I need to know what's right. And please, God, help me to accept Amy as just a friend. I don't want to hurt her, so please heal my heart and give me acceptance of her friendship and nothing more. Amen."

Silas had dreamed about Amy coming to him—dreamed that after he left she missed him so much that she jumped on the next train for Baxter. But it was just a dream, and Silas was going to have to accept the fact that she did not return his love.

True, he was going back in the fall, but he could not go expecting Amy to run into his arms. He had Amy's friendship, he hoped, and was going to work at keeping it. Every day he prayed for strength in this and knew God was already working. God had not deserted him, and Silas was determined to go on with his life.

Settled back into his work routine and doing well in his determination to move ahead, a few days later Silas saddled a horse in the late afternoon and went for a ride. He ended up down by the creek in the spot Julia had written about in her letter.

As Silas sat in this peaceful spot, he began to miss Julia so much he turned his mount toward the MacDonald farm. As he did so, he realized it would need to be a short visit as Christine would soon be getting supper on.

Silas was nearly on top of the farmhouse when he realized something was wrong: Julia and the boys were huddled together in the yard watching the house with fear-filled eyes. Spotting instantly the cause of their fear, Silas saw smoke coming from one of the kitchen windows.

"Mac's in there," Julia cried as Silas jumped from his mount. "He pushed us out when a pan on the stove caught fire.

Silas ran for the house, his heart pounding in fear, but Mac had things well under control. Silas began to throw the remaining windows open while Mac pulled singed curtains off a window near the stove.

Mac was not three steps out into the yard when Julia launched herself into his arms. Her body crashed against his with enough force to topple a smaller man.

Julia was nearly hysterical in her sobbing, and the boys clinging to their parents' legs were not much better off. Silas knelt down and hauled them into his arms. They accepted the comfort gladly and held on to his neck as the tears flowed freely.

While Julia was gaining some control, Mac released her to gather his boys into his arms. Silas looked on as they shared a family hug. His look then swung to the house. It would need to be aired out and that would take a few days.

There was little discussion as everyone seemed to be in a state of shock, but soon the wagon was hitched and Mac had his family loaded and on their way to Luke and Christine's. Silas had assured Julia that whatever needed to be done could wait until tomorrow.

Julia and the boys sat in the wagon, each with a bundle of clothes. Silas had ridden ahead, and Luke and Christine were in the yard as Mac drove the wagon in.

They saw instantly that Julia was white with strain. "Come on, Julia." Luke's voice was tender as he lifted her down.

As she looked up at her older brother, Julia's eyes filled with tears. "I thought Mac was going to burn."

"It's okay now," he said as he hugged her, his eyes meeting those of Mac who had been watching his wife with concern. "He's fine. You come inside. We'll take care of everything."

The four MacDonalds were swept inside and made comfortable. Julia seemed to be coming around, finally realizing Mac was really okay. Her eyes watched him as he went down the hall to clean up and change.

Over supper, Mac told briefly what had happened. The stove had been very hot and a greasy pan flared up without warning. Mac had grabbed the pan and moved it directly beneath the curtains. It all happened very fast and was enough to scare everyone and fill the downstairs with acrid smoke. The house would need a complete airing out and some minor surface work done in the kitchen.

Christine bustled about at bedtime making everyone comfortable. Silas was putting his two oldest nephews to bed, and Christine was checking on Julia. She was only in the bedroom a few minutes when the door reopened and Christine walked back down the hall and to the kitchen where Luke and Mac were talking.

"Excuse me a minute, Mac." Christine bent over her husband and whispered almost urgently for his ears alone, "Where are my nightgowns?"

Luke's eyes met Christine's and, though he tried to look innocent, she could see he was thoroughly enjoying this. Christine tried to look stern, but failed miserably. As they shared a long, loving look, both husband and wife were instantly back to a moment in one of the early weeks of their marriage.

Christine had just finished taking a bath in their bedroom near the stove, when she heard Luke coming down the hall. She searched quickly for a covering and grabbed the first garment she found—one of Luke's shirts.

Luke had entered and swept her with a look but said nothing. Christine had wondered about that look, but then put it out of her mind until the following night.

Luke was already snuggled beneath the covers when Christine came in to get ready for bed. She reached into her drawer for a fresh nightgown, but surprisingly only found a stack of Luke's shirts. She took one out and stood a moment in confusion. Understanding was not long in coming, and she turned to the man in the bed.

"Where are they?"

"Put away."

"Where?"

"You don't need them, Christie. Wear the shirt."

Christine fumed as she put the shirt on, determined to show him how ridiculous it looked. But once Christine was in the shirt, Luke only smiled.

Christine, indignant and angry, stomped over and stood by the bed. "It's indecent."

"What's indecent about it?" Luke found this highly amusing coming from a woman who went riding astride in her husband's denim pants, but wisely kept from commenting.

"My legs show." Christine looked down at the aforementioned members as though they themselves were the ones offended. The shirt stopped just above the knees.

"I know your legs show, but I'm the only one who will see them, so what's the problem?"

"LUKE!" Christine wailed in pure frustration, but it was no use. He was not about to tell.

Christine waited until the following day for Luke to leave the house. When he did, she tore the place apart. Every nook and cranny was searched. Nothing. She hadn't come up with a clue to where he had hidden her nightgowns.

Now husband and wife stood smiling warmly at each other. Julia needed a gown, and the story was too special to share. Luke arose, kissed his wife's cheek, and went to fetch a nightgown. Christine didn't follow him to the hiding place—she really didn't want to know.

31

Everyone spent the next few days working on Mac and Julia's house. They stayed nights at Luke and Christine's, but every minute of daylight was spent airing and cleaning. It was amazing how fast the smell of the smoke had infiltrated everything.

The first night Mac and Julia were back in their own home and the children put to bed, Mac turned his full attention to his wife for really the first time since the fire. He had sensed all along something was wrong but, with taking care of the house and the running of the farm, he'd had no time to talk with her.

"How are you doing?" They were sitting in the kitchen, each with a cup of coffee, and Mac was studying his wife's face with deep concentration.

"I'm fine." Julia answered with a small smile. The truth was that her head and back ached. But this, she was convinced, was due to the last few days.

"You don't seem fine."

"I don't?" Julia looked truly puzzled.

"No, you don't." Mac's voice was kind but firm.

"Well Mac, I feel a little achy and tired, but that's understandable after all that's gone on lately." Julia's voice told him she felt all of this was hardly worth mentioning.

Mac looked doubtful, and Julia reached for his hand. "I'm fine, honestly." Mac continued to look at her in unbelief, but he let the matter drop.

Over the next few days Mac kept a close watch on the woman he loved. She looked pale to him, but when he tried to talk with her about it, she burst into tears and said she was still a little upset from the fire. Anxiously he watched her, but he felt helpless since she seemed to think nothing was out of the ordinary. Mac prayed and tried to leave the

136

matter in God's hands, hoping he would know if and when to step in.

The time to step in came ten days after they returned to the house. Mac was in the barn when the boys came running from the house to tell him their mother was on the floor.

"She just fell over, Pa," Calvin said with fear as they followed their running father toward the house.

Julia was just coming to when Mac ran into the kitchen. He went down on the floor beside her and supported her as she tried to sit up. Her face was chalk white.

Julia opened her mouth to speak, but Mac cut in, his voice sharp with fear. "If you dare tell me you're fine, Julia, I'll throttle you."

That was exactly what she had been about to say and dutifully closed her mouth. Actually, she felt a bit nauseous and was glad to be still.

"Are you okay, Mom?" Charles' voice quivered with his question.

Julia turned to see her sons kneeling beside her, tears in their eyes. She started to reassure them, but Mac stepped in.

"Just as soon as your Uncle Mark sees her, we'll know."

"Oh Mac, I don't need—"

"Not a word, Julia. Boys, get the horses out. We're going to town." The boys had never moved faster to do his bidding.

Leaving Julia on the couch, Mac and the boys hitched the horses to the wagon. He threatened her with dire consequences if he found her off the couch or even sitting up.

Mac carried Julia to the wagon and tried to get her to lay down in the back, but she adamantly refused. Mac gave in just to get her to town as soon as possible.

Mac moved restlessly about Susanne's elegant living room as she sat helplessly and watched him. Julia had been with Mark in his office for over 30 minutes, and Mac was at his wits' end.

Inside the office, Mark looked at his sister, a little surprised she did not already know what he was about to tell her.

"Julia, you're pregnant."

"I'm what?"

"You are going to have a baby." Mark enunciated the words carefully as though speaking to a slow-witted child.

"But that's impossible."

Mark's eyebrows rose nearly to his hairline on that statement, but Julia rushed on. "I mean, I just never got pregnant after Charlie, and I just assumed that I couldn't." Julia's voice trailed off rather helplessly as she tried to take it all in. She was as surprised as Mark that she and Mac had not noticed any of the signs, for they had been there, staring them right in the face.

Mac! Julia's next thoughts were of her husband. She had to tell him right away.

The door leading from the office into the living room opened slowly, and Mac's entire body tensed as he watched his wife walk out followed by her brother. His peripheral vision caught Mark leading Susanne from the room, but his eyes were locked on Julia.

She walked toward him and without forewarning said, "I'm going to have a baby."

Mac's eyes closed, and he felt as if all the air had left his body. He stood a moment trying to pull air into his lungs. "Thank You, God. Thank You, God," his heart kept repeating.

When at last he opened his eyes, he pulled Julia tenderly into his arms. Julia felt him tremble, and her heart broke. He had been so frightened.

The boys found their parents in this embrace and, even though it was not an unusual sight, approached carefully.

When they broke apart, Calvin said, "Uncle Mark says you're okay and that you have good news."

Julia broke the news to them with tears in her eyes.

When Mark and Sue heard shouts and laughter from the living room, they knew it was alright to return.

What followed was a joyous chaos of laughter and tears. Mark took Julia back into his office to tell her how to take care of herself and things to watch for. She had never fainted when pregnant with the boys, and he intended to keep a careful eye upon her. He insisted Mac join them since he wanted his orders followed to the letter.

A while later Mac headed the wagon for Grandma Em's. Even with the boys fighting in the back over who would tell her the news, he thought this was probably the most beautiful day God had ever created.

32

The hour was late. Darkness had long since descended over the house. In the master bedroom Luke listened to Christine rustle and thrash about. She usually fell asleep instantly, and he wondered at her restlessness.

"Christine, what are you doing over there?" Luke asked when she shifted again and accidentally brought an elbow into his ribs.

"Oh, I'm sorry. Did I wake you?"

"No," he answered truthfully. "I haven't been to sleep yet. Why aren't you asleep?"

Silence greeted his question.

"Christine?"

"I'm worried about Si." She rolled over then and leaned over her husband. She could just make out his tanned face and dark hair against the whiteness of the pillow slip.

"Did you see the look on his face when Mac and Julia stopped to tell us about the baby? I know he's happy for them, but Luke, he wants a family of his own. I can tell. Something happened in Neillsville. I don't know what, but he's miserable and trying to hide it. We're not enough for him, nor should we be. He needs a wife and children of his own."

Luke reached up in the darkness and pulled Christine into his arms. He has noticed the changes in his brother. He could hardly miss them when they worked so closely. But Silas was a private person and Luke did not feel it was his place to question him.

With Silas, Luke, and Christine living in the same house, they had become very close. But some people did not express their feelings openly, and Silas was one of them. Especially if he was upset, he kept very much to himself. Luke could not step in unless he sensed an invitation from Silas.

Christine spoke again. "With Paul not living here, it's like he's the only one without a family of his own. Not only is everyone married, but everyone has children. And Luke," Christine paused, "I think I'm pregnant, too."

Luke's arms tightened around his wife's frame. "You think?"

"No, actually I'm sure." She didn't sound at all happy about it. Luke knew if Silas realized this, he would be angry.

They didn't talk anymore that night. Neither one had answers, and each tried to give their questions over to the One who did.

It was Saturday morning and the men had just come in for breakfast. Josh was clinging to Christine's skirt, and Luke rescued him so his mother could work.

When the four of them were seated, Silas gave thanks for the food. He ended his prayer by thanking God for never hiding His will and for His ever-abiding faithfulness.

Both Luke and Christine stared at him on the Amen and Silas announced, "I'm going to build a house."

"For whom?" Christine wanted to know.

"For me."

Christine looked at Luke and knew instantly this was no surprise to him. Silas could see a storm brewing and spoke up quickly. "I've been praying about it for some time. I really enjoyed the little bit of work we did at Mac and Julia's, and the cost and availability of building materials is very good right now. But most importantly, I feel God is telling me to build."

"Where will you build?" Christine's voice was small.

"On the far side of the big oaks."

"It's a pretty spot," Christine had to admit.

"Christine, don't look so sad. It's what I really want and besides, you'll need my room eventually when you give Josh brothers and sisters."

Christine blushed and looked down at her place. Silas' eyes flew to his brother's and Luke smiled a warm, "yes" kind of smile. Silas stared at Christine in shock.

"Silas, don't look so worried, I'm fine."

"Silas, don't look so worried, I'm fine." He imitated her voice in as high an octave as he could reach. He looked at her incredulously and spoke in his own voice.

"I can't believe you said that to me. First, Sue is sick to her stomach most of the day and losing weight, and then Julia decides to faint dead away on the kitchen floor, and now you ask me not to worry. Honestly, Christine, pregnant women scare me to death."

Luke and Christine could not hold their laughter at his chagrined tone, and he was not through.

"Sue I can handle because she's married to her doctor, but I'm still recovering from Julia. Now you go and spring this on me. I may not live through it." Silas' speech seemed to exhaust him for he slumped back in his seat and shook his head in despair. Luke and Christine only laughed all the harder.

Later that day Christine stood on the porch and watched her husband approach. He was moving entirely too slowly for her and she nearly shouted at him as she met him at the foot of the steps.

"Did you talk to him? Is he upset about something? If we've done something to make him feel unwanted, I'll never forgive myself. Why didn't he come to us and why didn't you tell me?"

"Christine, he only talked to me two days ago, and he still was not sure and didn't know when he would be. He's rather surprised to feel such a peace so quickly."

"But why didn't you tell me he was at least thinking of it?"

"Because there was nothing definite."

"Well, I don't know how that matters," Christine said and Luke only stared at her. "I am not overreacting." Luke continued to stare. "Well, I'm not." But her voice was losing its forcefulness. "I just worry about him and want him to be happy. I can't imagine him not living here."

"I know you care, but Christine I've never seen him so excited. He's like a kid with a new toy. And you know Silas would never do this on his own. If he said he prayed, he prayed."

Christine nodded and Luke hugged her. "God is taking care of Silas, Christine. Leave it in His hands."

33

God was indeed taking care of Silas. Although he could not yet think of Amy without feeling pain, he felt especially close to God at this time—as though his heavenly Father was giving him special comfort.

In no way did building a house take away the yearning for a wife, but it did serve to keep Silas' mind so occupied that the summer was slipping by and he was hardly aware of the passing of time.

The house materials had arrived and you would have thought it was Christmas as Luke and Silas inspected the goods.

Silas had fallen under the spell of a house he'd spotted in a mail-order catalog. The advertisement had described the house of his dreams with two stories and a total of four bedrooms. One of the bedrooms was on the first floor along with a front parlor, sitting room, dining room and a kitchen with a large pantry.

The dining room even had a built-in china cabinet. Silas had always admired the one built into the dining room of his grandparents' home—the house now owned by Mark and Susanne.

The second story sported three large bedrooms, all with spacious built-in closets. And at the top of the stairs was a huge linen closet.

There were special touches throughout the house, such as interior doors of soft pine in five-panel styling.

Silas' grin nearly split his face as he stood in the spot where he would build. Christine and Josh had joined him and Luke out beneath the oaks. Silas held his nephew in his arms and spoke.

"Right here, Josh. This is where I'll build my home—in the lee of these oaks." Christine felt tears sting her eyes upon hearing the hopeful excitement in his voice. "Please, God," she prayed, "make it special for Silas."

— ✛ —

The summer of 1889 was wonderful for crops, with just the right amount of rain and plenty of sunshine. The sunshine brought long hours of backbreaking work to someone building a house. On the other hand, the rain taught patience the hard way.

Silas paced on the front porch one rainy afternoon and stared out at the downpour. He knew it would not last long, but he felt a restlessness to be busy. Oh, there were things to be done in the barn—raising horses was a full-time job, but Silas wanted to build. It occurred to him, as he paced, that God had sent the rain and it was wrong of him to bemoan the fact.

Pausing from his restless walking, he wondered whether Grant's crops were getting plenty of rain and sunshine. Silas had found himself riding toward Mac's fields nearly every week, as if he could gauge Grant's progress by keeping tabs on his brother-in-law's crops.

It didn't rain all the time, and Silas worked hard in hopes of having the house complete by harvesttime. It felt good to walk through the house—even unfinished—and to imagine seeing it with furniture and homey touches.

Silas stood in the upstairs one day and looked at the three sizable rooms. "This is a lot of space for one man. What if I never have a wife, let alone kids?" Silas' mind could not stay the question. Just yesterday Christine, Julia, and Sue were talking about their pregnancies. He wondered if he'd ever see his wife grow with his child.

"God led you to build this house," Silas told himself. "And you're standing here wallowing in your own pity. Maybe you won't have a wife and kids, but that doesn't mean you won't be used of God. Maybe He will ask you to fill these rooms with orphans." Silas smiled at the thought and went back to work.

As it was, the house was not done when Mac started to bring in his crops. Luke had known all along what Silas' plans were for the fall, and so it came as no surprise to Luke when Silas told him he'd be writing a letter and leaving for Neillsville in a week.

34

Neillsville, Wisconsin

"I am not in love with Silas Cameron." Amy said the words to herself, but they didn't stop the furious pounding that started in her heart the moment she spotted him. Amy stood quietly and watched as he disembarked and crossed the platform toward her. He was so handsome. And then he was standing before her, smiling down in his sweet, gentle way, his height and the width of his shoulders blocking the sun.

"Hi." Suddenly shy, Amy's voice was hesitant.

"Hi yourself." Silas' eyes twinkled, and Amy knew that everything would be fine. She was the first one to reach and they hugged. It seemed to set the mood for the relationship they had both hoped to resume.

The ride out to the farm was filled with warm laughter and friendship. Silas was thrilled to be told that Grant was on his feet and strong but also looking forward to Silas' arrival. Amy said he was not a moment too soon; Grant had been in the fields for over a week.

Amy listened in quiet surprise to Silas' enthusiastic description of his new house. It sounded wonderful. She caught herself just before asking him if he was building a house because he'd found a girl this summer.

In fact, the summer for Amy had not been an easy one. Silas had not been far from her thoughts throughout his absence, and Amy honestly didn't understand why. For days she had thought about the way he had kissed her good-bye, and how she had allowed him to. Most of the time she had told herself it was because she felt guilt over not returning his love, and then pushed the thought aside.

But for Amy something was missing. She had never known discontentment before, never longed for things she did not have. But something was definitely missing. As the

summer aged, her frustration grew and she didn't understand why. She prayed long and hard over it, but specific
answers eluded her.

Amy still believed her father needed her on the farm, and
that he just didn't realize it. He had admitted how selfish it
would be if he expected her to give up her own life to take
care of him, but Amy didn't look at it that way.

She was positive that she was not building her life around
her father. The fact was he *did* need her. Amy found herself
thinking this so often that she wondered just who she was
trying to convince, herself or God.

"Your Aunt April and Uncle Chad send their love," Silas'
voice broke into her thoughts. "I talked with them soon
after I got home and told them how you were doing. And
then right before I left they had me to dinner on Sunday.
Your aunt sent you a present. It's in my bag."

"She wrote and said she had an early birthday present
for me."

"If I recall, your birthday is in November, same day as my
brother Paul's."

"Yes it is. Aunt April wrote about the gift. She said it was
fragile and hoped to send it with you. Intending it as a
wedding gift for me, she explained it had been in the family
for years. She also said she believes I will be married
someday and still wants me to have it." Amy's voice trailed
off at the end, unable to believe she had actually admitted
this, especially to Silas. She looked over to see Silas watching her, his expression unreadable.

Suddenly Amy felt indignant. "I don't know why everyone thinks I have to be married. Many people live long,
fulfilled lives and never take a spouse."

Surprised at her outburst, Silas was speechless. Amy
remained angry, and the rest of the ride home was made in
silence.

Silas stopped the wagon in front of the porch and jumped
down to assist Amy, but she sat quietly on the seat. He

stood looking up at her. Finally, without turning to him, her voice now subdued, she spoke.

"Silas, don't you ever sin?"

"Of course I sin." But Amy only turned and looked at him, clearly not believing his simple words.

"Just because I don't often lose my temper doesn't mean I never sin. Sins of the heart, Amy—the ones no one sees—can be the most serious of all. The sin of pride has brought me to my knees more times than I care to admit.

"I'm not perfect, Amy. Don't for a second think I am. I have my weaknesses." Something in Silas' voice on this last statement caused Amy to look at him in confusion, and Silas went on almost reluctantly. "Take Thomas Blane, for instance. I'm not sure what I would do if I ever met the man: shake his hand and thank him for stepping out of your life, or knock him to the ground for hurting you."

Amy's eyes widened in surprise at this violent talk coming from her Silas. *Her* Silas? What was she thinking?

"Silas!" The shout came from Grant who was moving toward them as fast as his still-healing leg would carry him. It effectively put an end to the conversation between the two young people.

Whatever was about to be said would have to wait. Silas reached quickly and lifted Amy to the ground before moving forward to meet Grant.

Amy breathed an unconscious sigh of relief. Once again she was spared the ordeal of dealing with her true feelings.

35

Amy stood in her bedroom holding the unopened package from her aunt. Silas had given it to her when he'd come down for supper, and even her father had looked at her strangely when she didn't immediately open it. There was no way to explain to Silas or her father, as there was no explaining even to herself about the almost desperate feeling within her to be alone to open this gift.

Amy's hands shook slightly as she peeled off the brown paper and unwrapped the gift. The package contained a beautiful glass berry dish. It was about eight inches in diameter and had an ornate A engraved on the side.

The note inside read: "I so want you to have this dish, Amy. It is a gift from my heart. The dish was given to me by my mother whose name was Agatha. She had received the gift from her mother, my grandmother, whose name was Adella. My name being April, the dish was passed to me and not to either of my sisters. With no daughter of my own, I feel it a privilege to pass this 'A' dish along to you, Amy. I hope someday I'll see it in your home on your own dining table. Love, Aunt April."

Amy took no note of the tears streaming down her face. To whom will you pass the dish, Amy? The question rolled around in her head as the tears continued down her cheeks and no answer came.

For the first time Amy was fearful of praying, fearful of facing God and what His will might be. Amy remained in her bedroom, alone and totally caught up in her pain.

"Do you think Amy's okay?" Grant and Silas were sitting on the front porch, and it bothered Silas that Amy hadn't joined them.

"I suppose she needed some time alone," Grant answered quietly.

"It's because I'm back." Silas' voice held regret.

"I imagine that does have something to do with it, Silas, but I think there's more to it. I'm afraid she didn't have an easy summer."

"Well, that's not surprising. She was pretty upset about your accident."

"You're right, she was very upset about that. But I think it's something else. My guess is, she's fighting God about something." Grant paused then and turned so he could look directly at Silas. "And I think that something is you."

Silas shifted uncomfortably in his seat, afraid of where this conversation was leading. He looked out across the yard, hoping Grant would take the hint and change the subject, but Grant wasn't through with him.

"Silas, I did break my leg, but there is nothing whatsoever the matter with my eyes. You're in love with my daughter. And when she stops looking at you like a big brother, she'll realize she loves you, too."

Silas stared at Grant in disbelief, and Grant went on. "Of course, you can't blame Amy for seeing you in that light. After all, you treat her like a sister. Maybe I'm wrong—maybe she is really nothing more than a sister to you."

"You're not wrong." Silas' voice was nearly inaudible.

"Well, then do something about it. In my day when a man fell in love with a woman, he courted her."

Silas could only gape at the man, hardly able to believe what he was hearing.

"Silas," Grant's voice was gentle now, "did you think I'd forgotten what it was like to be in love? I know it's not easy for you when you're living right here under the same roof. I suspect Amy knows of your feelings for her, but it's not at all convincing when you treat her with the same sisterly affection you always have."

Silas sat in silence for a moment before admitting in a

humble voice, "I've never courted a woman before. I'm not sure I'd know where to begin."

But Grant only smiled at him. "Silas, I have every confidence you'll come up with something."

Amy never did join the men on the porch that evening and Silas, knowing in the morning he'd be headed out to the fields, went to bed early. He had no trouble falling asleep, but as he waited for slumber to claim him, each second was spent thinking about all Grant had said.

36

The door slammed as Silas exited the kitchen. Amy stood near the table trying to decide if she had imagined what had just happened or if it had been real.

Her father and Silas had been outside working and Amy had washed the kitchen curtains. Stretching on the tip of her toes, she was rehanging them when she heard steps behind her and then Silas' hands covered her own. She let her own hands drop and he easily adjusted the rod, but she was unable to move with Silas directly at her back.

She thought nothing of this until Silas finished the job and made no move to step away. With his hands still high on the wall and his chest brushing her back, he bent his head slightly to the side and waited for Amy to look up at him.

When she did, he spoke as if there was nothing at all unusual about their stance. "Did you need help with anything else?"

"No." Amy's voice was higher-pitched than usual.

Silas moved then, bringing his face down until his nose nearly touched her temple. Amy stood frozen.

"Your hair smells nice." This said, Silas straightened. "Well, I best get back to work." Amy continued to stare at him as he sent her a warm smile and walked from the room.

Now she stood in bewilderment. Silas' attitude toward her the last few days had been different somehow, and Amy was thoroughly confused.

And her father—he had her completely baffled. If she didn't know better, she would swear he was matchmaking. But she just couldn't believe it of him.

It seemed that every time she turned around he was leaving her and Silas alone together. And twice he had requested certain dishes for supper, telling her they were Silas' favorites.

"Well," Amy said to the empty room, "I've got work to do. Men are just strange creatures and you have to learn to live with them."

Amy's decision to just "live with them" was fine when Silas was not around. But the truth was he had changed toward her, and she had no idea what to do about it.

For most of the day he was in the fields with her father, but those times when they were together, his actions could no longer be considered brotherly.

When he helped her in and out of the wagon, she noticed he held her just a moment longer than necessary. And when she did fix any of his favorite meals for supper, he didn't just thank her but kissed her right on the cheek— and in front of her father, too!

The real surprise came over three weeks after Silas arrived and right after he returned from a trip into town. Amy was dusting in the living room, wearing her oldest gown and her hair covered with a raggedy, faded scarf. She knew she had never looked worse.

"Amy, can you come outside a minute?"

"Oh Silas, you're back. Did you get everything from town?"

"I got everything on the list. Could you please come outside a moment? There's some—"

"Oh Silas, do we have company? I look terrible—this dress is filthy."

Silas could see he was going to get nowhere asking her. He walked toward her, took the dirty rag from her hand, and led her outside.

Amy followed mutely and listened while he spoke. "There was something in town I thought you might like. It's here in the back of the wagon. You don't have to keep it. I can take it back if you don't want it."

Silas led her to the back of the wagon and waited for her to look in. Seated upon a burlap sack was a tiny ball of black fur. Amy stared at the puppy, her mouth opening in a silent "oh." The sight of people brought the puppy to its legs, her miniature tail moving furiously, causing her entire body to vibrate.

"She looked like she needed someone to love her, and I thought you would be just the person."

"Oh Silas," Amy breathed as she gathered the wiggling little body into her arms. "She's darling."

The puppy must have agreed with Silas that Amy was the person to love her for she settled immediately into her arms and lay contentedly while Amy stroked her soft ears and head.

To Silas' surprise, Amy's face was wreathed in a smile but her eyes were shining with tears. Silas' heart overflowed with love for her and he took a step toward her, wanting with all of his heart to kiss her and declare himself.

Amy panicked when she saw his intent. "What shall we name her?" she nearly shouted at him and took a step backward. Silas looked at her for a moment as though he had no idea who she was talking about.

"The puppy, Silas, what shall we name the puppy?" Silas jerked as though stung, realizing what he had nearly done. His face flooded with color and, moving to unload the supplies to try and hide his embarrassment, he thought, "What a fool you are, Silas. Her liking the puppy doesn't change the way she feels about you."

"I'm glad you like the dog, Amy. I better get these things unloaded." Amy stood mute, not knowing what to say as he loaded a sack onto his shoulder. Silas evidently didn't feel words were necessary. As soon as his arms were full, he walked away without a word.

— ✤ —

"Another job? Are you sure?"

"That's what the note said."

"But we haven't heard from him all summer."

"I know, and we haven't had any money either."
"Are we doing it?"
"Yea, we'll do it. Maybe this time we'll see who he is."
"Yea, maybe. When do we go?"
"Tomorrow night."

37

Laughing, Amy watched with delight as Cocoa ran in small circles in front of her. Amy had just filled the dog's dish, but Cocoa wanted attention more than food, and Amy could not coax her into the stall she'd blocked off in the barn.

Amy decided to go into the stall and, as usual, Cocoa followed her. Amy felt almost guilty at tricking the dog, but as soon as Amy rushed out and pulled the plank back into place, the puppy headed to her dish.

Leaning lazily against a post, Amy thought back on the day before when Silas had brought the little dog home. That Silas had been about to kiss her had been more than evident and, the truth of the matter was, he had no right to such intimacies. But that didn't change the fact that she had panicked and responded badly, embarrassing them both.

Amy then remembered the stilted feelings between them just before Silas had gone home. Somehow knowing he would be returning in the fall had given Amy a sense of security. She didn't feel in a rush to right things between them, but now...

Being busy with the puppy the evening before had made conversation difficult, along with the fact that Silas was exhausted from the long day he'd put in.

But even considering Silas' physical state, Amy could not go to bed with things the way they were. Both men headed off to bed early, and Amy had found herself alone in the living room. With determination she marched halfway up the stairs and called to Silas through his closed door.

"Silas, can I talk to you a minute?"

The door opened after a moment and Amy headed down the stairs to wait. Silas approached almost warily, his face shuttered. Amy thought instantly of how many times she had hurt him—never intentionally, but hurt him nevertheless.

"I know you're tired, but I wanted to thank you for the puppy. She's adorable, and I already love her dearly. It was very thoughtful of you."

"You're more than welcome, Amy, and please let me apologize for doing things at times that make you uncomfortable."

Amy had not expected this and made no reply. She shifted uneasily under the intense stare Silas directed at her, but his eyes held her own. His hand lifted then and the backs of his fingers stroked ever-so-gently down her cheek. "Good night, sweetheart." His voice as gentle as his touch, he turned and went upstairs.

Now Amy stood gazing at Cocoa, thrilled to have the puppy, but totally unsure of how to deal with Silas and his feelings.

"Hello."

Amy jumped with surprise and turned as a strange male voice called to her from the doorway of the barn. She had to walk nearly the length of the barn to reach him, her look curious but friendly.

"Hello," the stranger said again as she approached. "I hope I'm on the right farm. My name is Paul Cameron; I'm looking for my brother Silas."

The first thing Amy noticed about the man was his height. The second was his voice. It was deep and perfectly modulated. The first comparison that came to her head was "smooth as honey."

Amy must have been staring because he spoke again, this time that perfect voice was filled with amusement.

"Is this the Nolan farm?"

"Oh yes, I'm sorry." Amy felt flustered and moved within arms' reach, her hand outstretched. "I'm Amy Nolan, and Silas is in the field with my dad."

"Good. I'm glad to know I have the right place. Maybe if you could point me in the right direction—"

"Oh certainly. You can go out, but they'll be in for supper anytime now if you just want to wait here at the house."

Centering her gaze on his evidently-new shoes, Amy thought, "They'll lose that shine very quickly if he walks all the way out to Silas and back."

"I'm not really dressed to go out, am I?" The amusement was back in his voice, and Amy looked up to see him smiling at her. "My word," she thought, "he's almost as good-looking as my Silas."

He was easily as tall, although his build was slighter, and his hair was just as dark, cut close to his well-shaped head. He was clean-shaven and Amy couldn't decide what was more appealing: his blue eyes with just a touch of green in them, or that full, smiling mouth filled with perfect white teeth.

Paul Cameron was doing some admiring of his own. Grandma Em had said there was someone special, but Silas had shared little with her and, other than the fact that the situation was not ideal, Gram knew next to nothing about the woman Silas loved.

Paul's first impression was how pretty she was—about Susanne's build, but her hair even more blonde. The dress she wore was a pale pink-and-white stripe. It seemed to put color in her cheeks even as her warm, blue eyes smiled kindly at him.

When Amy spoke, it was her turn to be amused. "Would you like to wait in the house?"

Paul grinned at her, totally undaunted by the fact that he'd been caught staring.

"Yes, Amy Nolan, I believe I will wait in the house. I hope my arrival won't put you out in any way."

"No, you're more than welcome. By the way, is Silas expecting you?"

"No," Paul answered as he held open the kitchen door. "I just made a surprise trip home to Baxter. It wouldn't have been a surprise if I had written ahead to see if everyone was home. I'm headed up north and, when I found out where Silas was, I decided I'd just stop in on the way."

"Well, I'm sure he'll be thrilled." Amy took his coat and bag and saw him settled in the living room with a cup of coffee. She then went to the kitchen to finish supper and Paul forced himself not to pace as he waited for the brother he longed to see.

38

Amy put a silencing finger to her lips as her father looked from her to the stranger standing in the doorway leading from the living room. Silas' head was still bent over the basin.

Paul watched his brother reach for a towel and vigorously rub his face and neck. Silas had just rehung the towel when, out of the corner of his eye, he caught sight of a fourth presence in the room.

At the first sight of his younger brother, Silas only stared, but then a slow smile began to break across his face. An answering smile was stretching across Paul's and, within seconds, the brothers were laughing and embracing, their words falling all over each other.

"When did you get here?"

"Your beard!"

"Have you been home?"

"Why didn't you write?"

"You look great!"

"So do you."

The men stopped trying to communicate and simply looked at one another and laughed. Silas took Paul's arm and led him further into the room.

"Grant, this is my brother Paul. Paul, this is Grant Nolan. And this," Silas' voice held pride, "is Amy. Have you met Amy?"

"Oh Si, you *have* got it bad," Paul thought as he studied the look on his brother's rapt face. "And I ought to know the signs."

Paul reached across the table to shake Grant's hand. "It's good to meet you, Mr. Nolan. And yes, Silas, Amy and I have met."

The two shared a smile and Amy said, "How about some supper?" The four of them talked and shared news during the meal and everyone left the table in good spirits. Silas hung back and insisted on helping Amy with the dishes.

"But Silas, you'll want to visit with your brother. He said he's leaving tomorrow."

"You're right, I do want to visit with him, but I also want him to hear you play, so I'm going to help you with these dishes so you can come out and entertain us."

"Oh Silas," Amy said, "I'm sure your brother doesn't want to hear me play. I'm sure he's heard countless piano players and I sincerely doubt he wants to hear another."

"Alright," Silas said, "I'll make a deal with you. My brother has always enjoyed hearing me play. If he asks me to play, then you're on. If he doesn't say a word, then I won't either."

"Deal," Amy said, and by the smile on Silas' face she knew she'd been had.

Amy would have loved knowing the actual amount of seconds it took Paul to ask Silas to play. Surprisingly, Silas didn't tease her at all.

"Well, Paul, I'd be only too glad to play, but you've never heard Amy play the piano and I know you would enjoy it."

Paul was sincerely delighted with the idea, and Amy cast an almost-shy smile at Silas as she moved to the keyboard.

The men sat quietly as Amy played, each one letting the music flow over him and basking in the sound of Amy's God-given talent. Grant's head lay on the back of his chair with his eyes closed, a slight smile on his lips.

Paul studied the small hands that moved so effortlessly over the keys and produced such celestial sounds, making him think of the way music might sound in heaven.

Silas' eyes never left Amy's face. He studied her lovely arched brows and the slight flush on her high cheekbones. His love found her flawless and lovely beyond compare.

Amy was nearing the end of a beautiful old hymn when she allowed herself to look about the room. Paul had joined Grant in tipping his head back and closing his eyes, but Silas was watching her, his expression loving.

Something inside of Amy began to open and grow, like a small flower beginning to bloom in the warm spring sun. "He's so wonderful and kind, and he loves me." The real truth of this fact hit Amy for the first time. The knowledge gave her such a warm, secure feeling she felt tears sting her eyes. Silas was God's child and she was God's child and together they could have a wonderful life with His blessing and beneath His watchful care. Unbidden upon the heels of this miraculous thought surfaced the doubts. "Could it really be that wonderful? Would he really love me for the rest of his life?"

Had Amy been able to tell Silas of her feelings and her fears, he would have answered all her questions and assured her of his love. But it was not to be on this night. With her father and Paul in the room, she knew there would be no time for talk. And when the evening came to an end, she had no choice but to head to bed with everything locked inside her. By morning she knew she would have talked herself out of approaching Silas.

— ✢ —

"We haven't shared a bed for a long time—do you snore?"

"It wouldn't matter if I did, little brother. This is my bed, keep that in mind."

"I take it that means you intend to hog the covers."

The men had just climbed into bed, and Silas tugged gently on the quilt in teasing. They lay quietly for a time, shifting once in a while for comfort, but neither one was close to sleep.

"Do you definitely have to leave tomorrow?"

"Afraid so. I'm already later than I said I would be."

"How many people in your congregation?"

"About 15, but the area has such potential, Silas. I just know God's going to use me up there." Paul's voice held all the enthusiasm he felt.

"I have no doubt He will, Paul, and you know I'll be praying."

"Thank you, Si. You know how much that means to me."
Silence fell again.

"Silas?"

"Yea."

"Do you want to talk about Amy?"

"How did you know?"

"Grandma Em and I talked. She didn't tell everyone, but we were discussing you and she shared what you had told her. Do you want to tell me?"

"I don't know, Paul. Amy is definitely my favorite subject, but sometimes I just can't see the point. She's just not interested in me."

"Are you sure of that, Silas? Are you sure she's not interested, or is it possible she's scared?"

"Scared of what?"

"Hasn't she been engaged before?"

"Yes, she has. The guy broke if off with her earlier this year."

"Why did he break if off?" Silas didn't answer. "Was it another girl?"

"I know what you're after, Paul, but she can't think I would do that to her."

"It doesn't appear to me that you really know what she's thinking. You haven't talked to her."

"When did you become such an expert?" Silas' voice was growing cross.

"I'm in love, too."

Silas said nothing for a long time, but questions were swarming through his head. He decided to pose his questions as Paul had done.

"Do you want to talk about her?"

Paul laughed. "I'm not sure you should get me started."

"Does she love you?"

"Yes." Paul's voice was apologetic, and Silas exploded.

"Paul! How could you think for one minute I wouldn't want your happiness?"

Following Silas' outburst, silence fell once again in the small attic room. Finally Paul said, "I'm not sorry she loves me, but it seems cruel to talk about my happiness when things are not settled between you and Amy."

"I appreciate your thoughts, Paul, but I think things are settled. I can't force her to love me, nor would I want to. I want her to come of her own accord—out of love, not pity or gratitude. Now please tell me about—"

"Corrine."

"Please tell me about Corrine—where you met, everything."

Paul's voice took on an almost dreamy quality as he spoke. "Her full name is Corrine Maria Templeton. I met her up north. She and her family are members of the church I'll be pastoring.

"We've really had very little time together, but I guess it was love at first sight. I was staying with her aunt and uncle while I was speaking up there, and we met when she came to see them.

"We would have had more time together, but she wasn't feeling very well and her dad insisted she go home. But it doesn't really matter. We had enough time to know how we feel about each other."

"So it's really serious."

"Is it ever! I want her for my wife. She loves God and is just as excited about the people and the work up there as I am. She's beautiful, too—tall like Christine, only very slim and willowy. Her hair is even lighter than your Amy's, almost a white blonde. I've never seen it down, but her aunt told me it's very long."

Paul's voice trailed off, and Silas was sure he was thinking of the woman he loved. Silas' thoughts were on the same track. "Your Amy," Paul had said. *"Your* Amy." He liked the sound of that.

"I can't give up, God," Silas prayed in his heart. "I love her so much. If there's even the slightest chance of us having a life together, I can't give up."

The brothers talked only a little while longer, a full day catching up with them. Tomorrow would bring good-byes which, though never easy, a good night's sleep would certainly help.

39

Amy's knife was putting the finishing touches on the chocolate cake she was frosting. The first thing her father had said upon seeing her puppy was, "She's as black as the cocoa you use to make my favorite cake." Amy thought the name very fitting and wasted no time in trying to come up with something better. Now, as Amy worked over the cake, she had to agree: The frosting was rich and indeed almost black in color.

She hoped Silas would enjoy it. He had taken Paul into town after breakfast to catch the train, and Amy had an inkling he might be upset or a little down when he got back. Realizing he was a little late now, Amy hoped everything was alright. She knew the cake certainly didn't make up for Paul's absence, but Amy wanted Silas to know she cared and was thinking of him.

About an hour later, Amy had really begun to wonder what had become of him when Silas drove quickly into the yard. Amy stepped onto the front porch in time to see Silas carrying Cocoa from the yard into the barn.

He was back out within seconds and striding quickly toward her, his face grave. As soon as he reached the porch, he took her hands and held them tightly in his own. Amy began to experience fear at his foreboding expression.

"Amy, I put Cocoa in the barn. I need to take you into town. As I drove Paul to the station, I could tell something was up. All through town I heard talk about your family. As soon as Paul's train left, I went straight to your uncle's. He was just on his way to get you. Your Aunt Bev is asking for you. She's been arrested for being connected with the robberies in the area."

All the color drained out of Amy's face upon hearing Silas' words. Swaying, she would have fallen but for his strong hands gripping her own.

"There must be a mistake." Amy's voice was little more than a thready whisper.

"I hope there is. Evan said she would talk to no one. The sheriff was kind enough to spare her the humiliation of the jailhouse, so she's at home with one of the town deputies."

Silas began to let go of Amy, intending to lead her into the house, but she clung to him. "Come inside, Amy. I need to go out and tell your dad. I'm sure he'll want to go with us." But still Amy would not let go of his hands.

"Please don't leave me, Silas."

Upon hearing the fear in her voice, Silas gathered her tenderly into his arms. He felt her tremble as he rested his cheek upon the top of her head. "It's okay, sweetheart. We'll go into town and get the whole story and I'll be right beside you."

God's hand was certainly on the Nolan family this day, for Silas looked over Amy's head to see Grant coming in from the fields. "Here comes your dad. Let's go tell him." Silas' large hand held Amy's as they walked past the barn to meet Grant. Silas told him all he knew and Grant insisted that Silas and Amy leave immediately.

"I'll saddle a horse and come in as soon as I clean up. If Bev is asking for you, then you need to get right in there."

Amy was nearly in a state of shock as Silas drove the team toward town. "Amy, I don't know what you're going to find when you get to your aunt's. But if she sees you so disturbed, it's just going to make her more upset than I'm sure she already is."

Silas' words penetrated Amy's painful confusion over this disastrous affair, and she started to pray. She began by thanking God for the fact that Bev had asked for her. This in itself was encouraging. Amy had prayed for years that by her word and deed her loved ones would come to understand their need for Christ and just maybe, as tragic as all of this was, it would be an open door to that end.

Amy spoke just as they entered the main street in town. "Thank you, Silas. I'm not sure what I would have done without you. If my Aunt Bev has no objections, will you come in with me?"

"I'll stay by your side as long as I'm able."

The scene in front of the Randall mansion was as close as Amy had ever come to living a real-life nightmare. Townspeople crowded everywhere. Snatches of conversations floated to the occupants of the wagon as Silas maneuvered the horses, attempting to skirt the crowd.

"If she's guilty she should be in the jail."

"The rich don't get treated like the rest of us do."

"I think she's been framed."

"It'd be easier to believe if it was him; he's certainly a cold fish."

"That's right, she just doesn't seem the type."

"Yea, she sure doesn't need the money."

Some of the sheriff's men and Bev Randall's two gardeners tried to restrain people as they trampled the landscape. Amy recognized one of the more zealous intruders as a man who worked for the town's newspaper. Unfortunately he spotted her at the same instant and began to run toward the wagon. Amy quickly directed Silas to drive to the back of the huge house. Again Amy felt God's hand on them when she saw that the guard at the back door was a man who had known her since childhood and immediately gave them entrance.

Two maids, both with swimming eyes and crushed handkerchiefs, were in the kitchen as Silas and Amy walked through. To save time, Amy headed for the back hall and stairway. The main staircase led directly to her aunt's room, but Amy was in a rush to get to the second floor and she nearly ran through the upstairs hallway to get to the spacious landing outside the master bedroom.

She stopped short, Silas nearly colliding with her, at the sight of a man standing at the door, a shining badge pinned smartly to the pocket of his shirt. His expression not at all welcoming.

Silas stepped in with the protective instincts of a mother bear. "This is Amy Nolan, Bev Randall's niece. I understand Mrs. Randall has asked for her."

The lawman eyed Silas' size for a moment before reluctantly opening the door and speaking quietly to someone within. Evan came through the door in the next second.

"Oh Amy, I'm so glad you're here. She won't talk to me." Amy had never seen her uncle so emotional, he was completely distraught. "All she'll say is 'I want to talk with Amy.'"

Amy nodded, and Evan stepped aside to let her in. Silas hesitated, but Evan gestured so he followed Amy. Evan closed the door from the outside.

Bev Randall stood in the small windowed alcove in the corner of the room and looked at the crowd below. Without turning, she spoke. "Thank you for coming, Amy. Is Silas with you?"

"Yes, he's here."

"Good. You need him. Please believe I never intended you should suffer for my conduct and mistakes. Of this I give you my word."

"So it's true you *are* involved in the robberies?"

"Yes, it's true. I hired the men who robbed those farms."

"Oh, Aunt Bev. Why?" Amy whispered in perplexity.

She turned and faced them. Silas thought she looked years older than the last time he'd seen her.

"I love Evan with all my heart. But I'm afraid the only love Evan has ever felt for anyone has been for you, Amy, and Maureen. At Christmas and on your birthdays I was allowed to spend lavishly on you. And I could buy anything for the house because, of course, a banker has a certain reputation to uphold. But never could I spend money for myself. I was never allowed anything of Evan's—not his love, his time, or his money.

"Oh yes, I have beautiful clothes to wear. But again, it's because I'm the banker's wife and we have an image to maintain.

"You wouldn't remember your mother's mother Amy, but a more wicked woman I've yet to meet. I was never allowed to forget I was not born a Randall. My family was poor and from a small town, 'hardly more than a dot on the map,' she used to enjoy reminding me."

"But Aunt Bev, he must love you. Or else why would he have married you?"

"I've often wondered that myself. I think he had just decided it was time to marry and I was in the right place at the right time. But then maybe he did love me and I killed that love because I could never give him children."

"But Aunt Bev, I still don't understand about the robberies."

"It's simple really—I wanted the money. I was sick to death of having to beg Evan for every dime I needed. Sick of being questioned about what I was spending." She gave a short, humorless laugh and turned back to the window. "The funny thing is I really believed no one would ever know."

There was a knock on the door then and Silas answered it. Grant stood on the threshold, his hat in his hands. Evan was behind him.

"Who is it, Silas?"

"It's me—Grant, Bev. Can I come in?"

She nodded and Silas swung the door wide. Somehow Silas seemed to sense their need to be alone, and he took Amy's arm and they walked from the room.

Evan was still on the landing as the door closed behind Grant and Bev. "Uncle Evan, we need to talk." Evan nodded and the young people followed him downstairs to the library.

40

Evan Randall was a proud man. It showed in his carriage, the way he spoke, and in nearly every facet of his life. But today as he faced his niece in the small library downstairs, he looked like a beaten man.

He motioned Amy and Silas into chairs, but he remained standing. "Please tell me what she said." Amy hesitated, so Evan said, "I'm sure she's upset with me or she would have talked directly to me."

Amy didn't see that she had any choice. She looked to Silas, and he gave her a small nod. Quietly and as gently as possible, Amy relayed what her aunt had shared.

Evan dropped heavily into a chair and stared at her in disbelief. "I had no idea. You mean she actually believes I don't love her?" Amy gave a small nod and fought to keep the tears at bay, his expression so clearly showing his hurt and confusion.

"Did she really say that about the money?" Again Amy nodded. "I never intended that she feel she couldn't have money. I certainly never denied her."

"But you do question her?"

"Yes, I guess I do," he admitted with a heavy sigh. "But I honestly never meant to be stingy with her or make her think I didn't care."

Other than the sound of the townspeople out front, the house was still. There were no other words to be said in the library downstairs. And the occupants of the room sat and wondered what was being said upstairs in the master bedroom.

Bev had turned back to the window, and Grant was not sure what to say or even what had led him to come into the room this way. He had not been at all prepared for the mob out front and he was still reeling with shock over the severity of Bev's circumstances.

"I'm glad you came, Grant. I asked for Amy because I guess she feels like the daughter I never had and felt I needed to see her to say—"

Grant was afraid of what she was going to say. Her voice sounded terribly despondent, which concerned him.

"I've shamed Evan, you know. He didn't deserve this. He won't be able to show his face in this town. It would be better for him if I were dead."

"You're wrong, Bev." Grant's voice was emphatic. "No one wishes you dead, and especially not Evan. I realize he's not demonstrative, but I know he cares for you. He's proud of the position you hold in this town and the work you do."

Bev only shook her head sadly and turned from the window. "I know you mean well, Grant, but—"

"No, Bev, I'm not saying these words to ease your conscience. Your involvement in these thefts was wrong, but it doesn't mean your life is over."

"You know, don't you, Grant? I asked for Amy so I could say good-bye. Evan keeps a small-caliber pistol in the closet. I haven't talked to him and he doesn't understand, but the truth is I just couldn't face him after what I've done. He's not perfect, but at least he's not a liar and a thief. I've shamed the Randall name."

"It's true, Bev, that what you did was against the law, and you have no choice but to face the judge with your crimes. But Bev, there is an area in your life where you do have a choice. How will you face God, Bev? Will He be your Judge or your Savior?"

"Grant, how can you speak to me about facing God after what I've done?" Bev cried. "It's blasphemous! I'm dirty, Grant! Maybe at one time God would have welcomed me, but I'm sure He wants nothing to do with me now."

"You're wrong, Bev, so wrong. God sent His Son, Jesus Christ, to die for the dirty, the wrong, the sinful. If we were able to cleanse ourselves before coming to Him, we wouldn't need Him. Listen to me, Bev. I may not have taken money from anyone, but without the saving knowledge of Christ I would still be headed to hell."

The harshness of his words fell on Bev's mind like the blow from a hammer. "Yes," she thought, "what I'm going through right now is awful, but there *is* worse—there's eternity without God." Bev Randall believed in an afterlife, and she knew she was not ready to face it.

Bev sank onto the edge of the bed and Grant pulled a chair close. "Bev, the Bible says all have sinned and fall short of God's glory. It also says there is hope for man in the form of Christ Jesus. He died, Bev, for the sins that make you feel so dirty. And the Bible says you need only believe on Him to know His saving grace."

"Oh Grant, I just don't know. I haven't prayed since I was a little child at my grandmother's knee."

"Bev, come as you are to Jesus Christ who loved you enough to die for you. 'For God so loved the world, that he gave his only begotten Son, that whosoever believeth in him should not perish, but have everlasting life.'"

Bev looked at Grant and tears swam in her eyes. "Please help me." She sounded like a helpless child, and Grant knew it was time. Bev Randall was ready to put her hand in God's.

"It's so simple, Bev. Just repeat after me and take God at His word." Bev nodded, and Grant began. "Dear God in heaven, I know I have sinned and I'm not worthy of Your love. But I believe, God, that You died for my sins and I now give them to You. Please take my life in Your hands, Lord. And thank You for saving me."

Bev dutifully repeated each sentence Grant spoke, and then Grant prayed when she was through. "Dear God, thank You for Your love and the miracle You have brought today in Bev's life. Please God, stay with her as she faces the rough days ahead. Help her to remember that she is now Your child and You'll be beside her. I praise You for Your Son, Jesus Christ, and His death for us. Amen."

Grant and Bev lifted their heads simultaneously and looked at one another. The crowd could still be heard outside, and there was movement at the door as though the guard outside had shifted against it.

The sounds were only half-heard by the two people within as they concentrated on the life-changing miracle that had just occurred in Bev Randall's heart.

When Grant broke the silence, his voice was gentle and reverent.

"Bev, if you believe what you just prayed, that Christ *did* die for you, then you're now His child."

Bev clasped her hands together, trembling with excitement, her voice little more than a whisper.

"Oh Grant, it's not so scary now. I still have to face what I've done, but I don't feel so alone."

The two adults stood, and Grant gave Bev a hug. He felt a bit awkward, but Bev was smiling when they parted. Grant needed to share one last thing. "You know, Bev, Maureen loved you deeply. She prayed daily that you and Evan would come to know her Savior."

"I hope she knows now."

"I'm sure she must be singing right along with the angels."

A knock sounded and Bev called for the door to be opened. Evan came in hesitantly. "Evan," Bev's voice was more gentle than he'd heard in years, "I need to talk with you."

Grant went out the door to find Silas and Amy waiting for him. They each had a final look within before the guard firmly closed the door. Evan and Bev were seated on the bed, Evan's arm was around his wife, her head resting on his shoulder. They could hear her talking quietly, but without hesitation or fear.

Grant could see that Silas and Amy were full of questions, but now was not the time or place. They made their way through the house and, with most of the crowd gone, were soon headed for home.

41

Amy woke up feeling rested for the first time since Silas came back from town with the news of her Aunt Bev. The night they arrived home, milking and chores awaited them, but over supper each shared what they had seen and heard.

Amy wept openly upon hearing of her aunt's salvation. Grant had asked Silas to lead them in prayer for Evan, whose heart had never made that step.

Grant had gone into town again the following day and returned with a lengthy report. He had seen Bev and Evan who were both holding up well and had had a long talk about the robberies with the sheriff.

The sheriff cleared up many questions and, once back at the farm, Grant relayed the information to Silas and his daughter. The discovery of who was actually behind the crimes was brought to light within hours of the Cooper brothers being arrested for the last robbery.

The men did not hold up well under questioning and soon told of the notes left for them in an old tree outside of town. Since all the notes had been saved, the sheriff could see he'd been in error in the way he'd reassured the towns-people. Every slip of paper pointed to someone at Evan's bank being involved.

In a short time the sheriff had brought in a young bank teller and it was this person who confessed to delivering "off the record" reports to the banker's home three times a week.

With this information, along with the brothers' description of the unidentified black-cloaked rider who always made the money exchange, the sheriff had soon been on his way to arrest Evan Randall.

It was Bev who gave herself away—not that she would have allowed Evan to take the blame, in any case. When the

sheriff arrived, Evan had been out and Bev had just immediately assumed she'd been discovered. The sheriff had
relayed his conversation with Bev to Grant:

"I can't say as I'm glad to see you, Mitchell."
"Then you know why I'm here?" the man
asked, truly saddened at his findings.
"Yes, I know why you're here. You know, I
really believed I would get away with it. I kept
things so simple, so few people involved. I even
made the money exchanges myself."

Bev, upon seeing the lawman's stunned face, soon realized her mistake. The sheriff had no choice but to report all
he knew and, late as it was, it didn't take long for all of
Neillsville to hear.

Silas and Grant with their work in the fields had dealt
with the news better than Amy who suddenly had time on
her hands as she alternately prayed and worried over all
that had ensued. And always at the back of her mind was
the knowledge that the crops were nearly in and Silas
would be leaving.

42

Silas' thoughts were identical to Amy's. "The crops are in. Another day and I need to go home, and this time I have no reason to come back." Silas wanted to weep just thinking about it. He found himself practically begging God to give him some time with Amy.

Certain that he knew how she felt, Silas just needed to talk with her for a spell. It might be the last time for quite a while. The time came that very morning, the day before he was scheduled to leave.

The weather was turning cold and, after spending days with canning and putting her garden up, along with the stress of Bev's pain, Amy felt a desperate need to be outdoors before winter set in and made being out miserable.

The big oaks at the top of the bluff looked inviting, and Amy bundled herself from head to toe and set out for her favorite spot. She had been sitting on a fallen log for less than half an hour when Silas joined her.

They sat in companionable silence for a time, both feeling good that talk wasn't needed. The surrounding bluffs and farms stretched out before them, almost creating a valley. From their vantage point it was hard to believe there was life beyond the houses and fields they could see. And with the world so quiet and cold on this morning, it was even harder to believe people were hurting and life was not peaceful for everyone.

Silas eventually turned his head from the view and looked at Amy's profile. Amy, feeling his look, turned and let her eyes meet his.

"I'm leaving tomorrow." Silas didn't know why he said it; she already knew.

"I'll miss you."

"Will you, Amy? Will you really?"

Her heart ached at hearing the wistfulness in his voice and she answered very gently, "Yes, I'll miss you very much."

She continued to look at him, and Silas believed he would drown in the crystal-clear blue of her eyes. As before at the train station, he moved slowly, giving her plenty of time to see his intent and draw away.

Amy's heart melted within her as his lips touched hers, and Silas felt as though his own heart was going to pound through his coat as she leaned closer and didn't pull away.

One second they were kissing and the next second Amy was gone. Silas stared up at her from his place on the log. She had leapt up and was staring at him with tortured eyes, her hands clenched so tightly together that her knuckles were white. Silas stood and reached for her as he spoke.

"Amy, please—"

"Don't touch me, Silas—just don't touch me."

Standing in front of the log and holding his place, Silas spoke. "Amy, you must know how I feel. You must know that my feelings for you are deep. And you, Amy, what about you? Please don't ask me to believe you don't feel anything for me."

"Of course I feel something for you. We're friends." the words sounded foolish and inane even to her own ears, but Amy couldn't seem to help herself.

Silas looked furious. "Is that what you were just now when you let me kiss you—a friend?"

Amy shrugged helplessly, not even knowing herself why she had allowed the kiss. Silas drug off his cap and Amy watched him rake his hand through his hair, his frustration more than evident. Suddenly Amy felt angry and frustrated, too.

Taking him completely by surprise, Amy boldly stepped forward and pushed as hard as she could on his chest. Normally he would have hardly noticed the relatively slight pressure she put on him, but he was so surprised by her action that he took a step backward, forgot the log, and fell over it and onto his back.

"What did you do that for?" he bellowed from his undignified sprawl on the ground.

"Because you've ruined everything. We were such good friends, and you've just ruined it," Amy cried in pure frustration.

Silas was off the ground in an instant, knowing his brother Paul had been right. Even as Amy had shouted at him in rage, he had seen the fear written across her face.

Amy retreated as he came toward her, and Silas stalked her until she was backed up against a tree. His expression was fierce but his voice was calm. "Take a good look at me, Amy Nolan, a very good look. I am *not* Thomas Blane. I am *not* going to declare my love for you and then marry someone else."

Silas' look grew extremely tender as they both stood still, his eyes drinking in the woman he loved. He cupped her face within his big hands before he spoke his next words. "I love you, Amy. I love you as I've never loved anyone. You would but need to crook your smallest finger in my direction and I would gladly carry you down this hill to the parsonage and make you my wife today."

Silas felt as if a giant hand had reached into his chest and was attempting to squeeze the life out of his heart, so great was his disappointment when Amy did not respond to his avowal of love.

Silas straightened and moved a few steps away from Amy, his voice, if not his face, betraying his anguish. "I'll be taking one of your horses to the train in the morning. I'll leave it with the livery nearest the depot."

Turning as though he would walk back to the house, Silas hesitated. Amy hadn't moved away from the tree, and Silas didn't look at her as he spoke.

"Long after I get home I'll love you. If by some miracle you realize you can return that love, know that I'll welcome you with open arms and an open heart."

Amy was very cold inside and out by the time she followed Silas down the bluff and back to the house. And for the first time she could ever remember, she did not feel like singing at the sight of her home.

43

Silas sat aboard a southbound train, his gaze centered out the window, seeing nothing. It was actually over, and Silas was still coming to grips with the fact. Right up to the time he left, he believed Amy would come to him. There was no way she was indifferent to his love, of that he was sure. But the decision had to be hers. Even if he could force her, he wouldn't want to.

The rest of the day after they had come back off the bluff had been awkward and painful. Silas found himself wishing he'd planned to leave that day. He knew Grant had figured out the problem and had compassionately said little.

In the evening not long after supper, Silas' mind was already making plans to turn in early. Grant had other ideas and asked Amy to play. Silas wouldn't have cared what the circumstances were—he would not have missed that.

As Silas brought the evening to mind, he wondered if Grant had planned it all along.

"Amy, will you play that song you wrote for me?"

"The music is in my room," Amy answered, obviously reluctant.

"Well, we'll wait for you."

The men did wait, and Amy was only a few notes into the piece when Grant interrupted her. "Please sing it, Amy."

She looked at her father for a long moment and then finally nodded. Grant said to Silas, "Amy put a poem she'd written to music this summer and gave it to me when I was laid up. She titled it 'My Rock, Refuge and Savior'."

As soon as Grant had finished his explanation, Amy played and sang. Even aboard the train, the seat uncomfortable, the air stale, and the passengers noisy, Silas had only to close his eyes to see her and hear her voice.

My Rock, Refuge and Savior

Words by Lori Wick

Music by Timothy Barsness

"Beautiful," Silas thought as his mind's eye brought up the images of how she looked and sounded. "Please God," Silas prayed as the train moved down the track for home, "please be my Rock, Refuge, and Savior and bigger than the hurt within me because she's not at my side."

44

The chill of winter was descending on Baxter in a no-nonsense way, and Silas was thankful the roof was on his house and his stoves in the kitchen and living room were piped in and working.

He was not completely finished with the house and had yet to stay a night in it, but the remaining jobs were small and rather fun, and Silas had found that the time spent on the house was a much-needed balm upon his wounded emotions.

Luke had not worked on the house at all while Silas was absent, mostly for the sake of time since he was called upon, once again, to carry the load of both men. But Luke was wise, and also held back for the simple reason that if he were building a home, he knew he would want to do the majority of the work himself.

So the house awaited Silas. Even as he worked, he harbored in his heart a faint hope, as he had before, that Amy would miss him and come on the next train. But as the days turned into weeks, Silas was forced to accept the fact that she was not going to come.

He continued to feel God's presence and to trust in Him daily for strength, but to anyone who knew Silas well, it was obvious some of the sparkle had dimmed in his royal-blue eyes.

There was even a certain young woman at church, newly widowed, with two small children. Silas thought of offering his hand, knowing that she needed someone, and thinking in time they might even learn to love each other. But he didn't entertain the idea for long; he knew it was not what God would have him do.

Thanksgiving had just passed, and Silas had found the day nearly unbearable. The women were constantly laughing about the changes in their shapes, and Mac was so gentle with Julia that it made Silas' throat ache just to watch them.

There were days when he thought he'd made a mistake about the job offer from Frank Chambers. But as always he prayed and God would show him small, but sound reasons for staying.

The main reason for staying finally came. She arrived by train in Baxter wearing new clothing from her hat to her shoes. She knew the way to her aunt and uncle's and headed directly there.

She resisted her Aunt April's attempts to persuade her to come inside and warm herself by the fire, stating simply, "Thank you, Aunt April, but I need directions to Silas' house."

April Nolan wasted no time in asking for explanations, and soon Amy could be seen in the beat-up buggy from the livery, headed out of town with the wind blowing a cold blush on her cheeks.

Silas was in one of the upstairs bedrooms when he spotted the rented buggy with its one brown horse loping over the lightly snow-covered ground. He watched for a moment and almost turned away until he realized the buggy was not headed to Luke and Christine's, but to his house.

Amy was out of the buggy and looking at the huge farmhouse which loomed above her by the time Silas arrived in the yard. He approached her with a look of wonder on his face, heedless of the small flakes of snow that fell on his shirt, his coat forgotten inside the house by the front door.

"Your house is beautiful."

"Thank you, I'm glad you like it."

Silence fell with the snow.

"How's your dad?"

"He's fine. He said to tell you hello."

"Good."

The silence was longer this time. Silas looked at the woman before him, the blue of her hat a perfect frame for her lovely face and hair. He'd forgotten how breathless he became whenever she was near.

In the same state, Amy drank in his size and the way the snow looked on his dark hair. Her breath made smoky little puffs in the air, and she thought she would cry if he didn't hold her soon. Finally he spoke.

"Amy, I think I'd better tell you, if you're not here for the reason I hope you're here, you'd best say so, because you're about two seconds away from being kissed."

"Oh Silas, please don't wait two whole seconds."

Luke had seen the buggy, too, and with innocent curiosity had just rounded the biggest oak to find his brother with a petite blonde crushed in his embrace. It was obvious neither one was aware of the snow covering them or that the woman's hat lay on the ground beside them.

Luke turned and headed back to his own house, hoping Silas would bring her over to meet them. Silas had been back for weeks, but Luke was sure he'd just now arrived home.

Epilogue

Neillsville, Wisconsin
Spring 1890

Amy Cameron stood beneath the big oaks, not really focused in on the beautiful view. The position of the barn blocked the house, but Amy knew it was there. Her father and her husband were down in the house, supper was over, and they were discussing the planting. Her husband. Amy felt a chill go through her each time she thought the words.

It was just a year before that she and Silas had faced each other in the barn on a very rainy night. Little did she know how her life would change with the break in her father's leg and Silas' arrival. And to think she had almost ignored God's leading and let him get away.

But she had been so afraid, so afraid of being hurt again. True, Thomas and Silas were nothing alike, but there was yet another factor. Amy had not wanted to believe her father could live without her. Even as Silas had shared about his own struggle with pride, pride had brought Amy to her knees. She had known the day he left it had been a mistake. But Amy would not listen to her heart, and over the next few weeks had become more and more miserable.

It was Grant who turned things around. Amy found her gentle, kind-spoken father furious with her.

"Look at you!" he had shouted at her. "You're pale and losing weight, and for what? To stay here and take care of me when the man you love is waiting to share his life with you?"

Amy had stared at him, her mouth opened wide. But Grant wasn't done yet.

"I've never thought your skull thick, Amy, but I'm beginning to think it's going to take an oak beam along the side of your head before you see the truth. You're fighting God in this, and what you're fighting is your very own happiness. You've hurt Silas terribly and, to be very frank, I'm ashamed of you."

Amy stood on the bluff remembering his words and how they had hurt. Her father had held her and she'd cried, knowing he was right.

Thanksgiving had come and, to the astonishment of the Nolans, they had been invited to the Randall mansion. Bev had come before the judge soon after Silas left, and many had complained about the privileges of the rich when they heard about how light her sentence was—almost nonexistent. They were somewhat mollified over the high fines she was ordered to pay. The judge had ruled that Bev pay over double what had been taken from the different farms.

Only Grant and Amy had understood Aunt Bev's joy in this order when on Thanksgiving she had told them the news with tears in her eyes.

Amy now reflected on that time. The day had been a good one, but Silas was most definitely missing. Now, however, they were husband and wife, and at the moment Amy could come up with only one cloud on the horizon.

Even as she thought of it, tears stung her eyes. Silas picked that moment to join his wife on the bluff. Amy didn't turn, and Silas' arms came around her from behind, his chin resting atop her soft, blonde hair.

Silas heard Amy sniff. "Talk to me, Amy."

"I'm not pregnant."

Silas began to wish he'd never shared with Amy his great desire to fill their house with children. She was bound and determined to give him a child in their first year of marriage. And though many families started this way, it certainly wasn't written anywhere that this and this only was the correct procedure.

"Amy, we'll have children. I promise you."

"Silas, how can you possibly make such a promise?"

"Well," he thought a minute, "if we don't have children of our own, we'll take in a bunch of orphans."

"Do you really feel that way?" Amy turned in his arms so she could see his face. "Would it really not bother you if I couldn't give you children?"

"It really wouldn't bother me. God gave me you, and that's what's most important to me."

Amy smiled up at him in relief and he pressed a kiss to her forehead. "We need to go back to the house and spend more time with your dad. This visit has gone by too fast; we're headed home tomorrow."

Amy nodded, not at all upset with the idea of leaving for Baxter. Envisioning the house where she and Silas had lived as husband and wife for over five months, she linked her arm through his for the walk down the hill and began to sing.

About the Author

Lori Wick is one of the most versatile Christian fiction writers on the market today. From pioneer fiction to a series set in Victorian England to contemporary writing, Lori's books (over 1 million copies in print) are perennial favorites with readers. The Place Called Home series is a heartwarming saga of faith and love in the farmlands of Wisconsin. Born and raised in Santa Rosa, California, Lori met her husband, Bob, while in Bible college. They and their three children, Timothy, Matthew, and Abigail, make their home in Wisconsin.

Lisa Samson
THE HIGHLANDERS
The Highlander and His Lady
The Legend of Robin Brodie
The Temptation of Aaron Campbell

THE ABBEY
Conquered Heart

Ellen Gunderson Traylor
BIBLICAL NOVELS
Esther
Joseph
Joshua
Moses
Samson
Jerusalem—the City of God
Melchizedek

Dear Reader:

We would appreciate hearing from you regarding this Harvest House fiction book. It will enable us to continue to give you the best in Christian publishing.

1. What most influenced you to purchase *A Song for Silas*?
   - ☐ Author
   - ☐ Subject matter
   - ☐ Backcover copy
   - ☐ Recommendations
   - ☐ Cover/Title
   - ☐ _____

2. Where did you purchase this book?
   - ☐ Christian bookstore
   - ☐ General bookstore
   - ☐ Department store
   - ☐ Grocery store
   - ☐ Other

3. Your overall rating of this book:
   ☐ Excellent ☐ Very good ☐ Good ☐ Fair ☐ Poor

4. How likely would you be to purchase other books by this author?
   - ☐ Very likely
   - ☐ Somewhat likely
   - ☐ Not very likely
   - ☐ Not at all

5. What types of books most interest you? (Check all that apply.)
   - ☐ Women's Books
   - ☐ Marriage Books
   - ☐ Current Issues
   - ☐ Christian Living
   - ☐ Bible Studies
   - ☐ Fiction
   - ☐ Biographies
   - ☐ Children's Books
   - ☐ Youth Books
   - ☐ Other _____

6. Please check the box next to your age group.
   - ☐ Under 18
   - ☐ 18-24
   - ☐ 25-34
   - ☐ 35-44
   - ☐ 45-54
   - ☐ 55 and over

Mail to: Editorial Director
Harvest House Publishers
1075 Arrowsmith
Eugene, OR 97402

Name _____

Address _____

City _____ State _____ Zip _____

**Thank you for helping us
to help you in future publications!**